WASTED

A Love Story / A Mystery

FICTION

BY
DUKE TIPTON

Order this book online at www.trafford.com
or email orders@trafford.com

Most Trafford titles are also available at major online book retailers.

Printed in the United States of America.

ISBN: 978-1-4269-4212-9 (sc)
ISBN: 978-1-4269-4213-6 (e)

*Our mission is to efficiently provide the world's finest, most comprehensive book publishing
service, enabling every author to experience success. To find out how to publish your book,
your way, and have it available worldwide, visit us online at www.trafford.com*

Trafford rev. 09/25/2010

 www.trafford.com

North America & international
toll-free: 1 888 232 4444 (USA & Canada)
phone: 250 383 6864 ♦ fax: 812 355 4082

WASTED
A Love Story / A Mystery

Synopsis

This is a fictional story of a beautiful girl who was raped by her older brother. The Child Protective Agency placed Lisa in a group foster home, where the other female residents abused her.

Lisa took a job at an outdoor restaurant and concert venue (this was against the state laws for foster-home residents) and fell in love with her older boss. The boss took Lisa on a cruise to the Baja peninsula, Mexico. On the cruise, Lisa met a slick, fast-talking gentleman and exposed her breast to him. Lisa's jealous lover caught them in the act.

The fast-talking man turned out to be married, and Lisa could not go to his room. The jealous lover would not let Lisa return to his room ... Lisa was on a cruise ship in the middle of the ocean. What could she do?

A little Vietnamese man spotted Lisa in the water as he watched the wake from the back of the ship. When Lisa was discovered in the water, the ship was traveling at a rate of twenty-eight knots.

A search by the ship's crew had negative results. The U.S. Coast Guard was able to retrieve Lisa's body. Detectives were flown to the ship from Los Angeles. The detectives conducted a thorough investigation, but they were unable to determine why Lisa was in the water.

Anna Lee, Clifford, and Roger Cole

This story is about the wasted life of a beautiful sixteen-year-old girl named Lisa Marie Cole.

Lisa had an eighteen-year-old brother, an alcoholic father, and a gambling addict mother. Her brother, Roger, did all the housekeeping, yard work, grocery shopping, meal preparation, and property maintenance. Lisa's father, Clifford Cole, was a night watchman at a consolidated warehouse on the edge of town.

A computer-device manufacturer used the consolidated warehouse to hold its excess inventory. These memory devices went into very large mainframe computers. These memory devices were extremely fast, as they had to retrieve bits of data from trillions of stored bytes in less than one microsecond. In order to accomplish this task, a large amount of pure gold was used in all of the buss bars.

To feed his alcohol addiction, Cliff would open the sealed shipping containers of memory devices and remove the gold-laden prizes. He would then sell the devices to a gold broker, who melted down the device to retrieve the gold. After removing the device from its shipping carton, Cliff would carefully replace all of the packing material and repair the seal. He would then place the pilfered carton on very the bottom stack of shipping cartons. Cliff's gold broker would meet him at the warehouse. Many times Cliff would trade the gold-laden device for liquor, without bothering to ask for money.

Every day, Cliff carried the dinner that Lisa's brother had prepared to work in a metal lunch box. He was able to install a bottle of booze in the lunch box as well. Cliff was always half soused when he arrived home. He had a large La-Z-Boy recliner at the far end of the living room. After dinner, he propped himself up in the chair with a drink in his hand and dozed off. The routine changed somewhat on the weekends: Cliff would read the newspaper in his big reclining chair with a drink in his hand. A reading lamp stood behind the chair. The lamp was a simple pole resting on the floor with a flexible gooseneck that held a single screw-in light socket.

No lampshade shielded the reading lamp. The light from the reading lamp eliminated all surrounding objects.

One Saturday evening, the electric bulb in Cliff's reading lamp burned out. He did a thorough search throughout the house for a replacement lightbulb. He looked high and low, but no replacement lightbulb could be located at the house. In desperation, Cliff went outside to the back patio and unscrewed the large security lightbulb from its fixture. He took the 300-watt lightbulb into the house and screwed it into his reading lamp. This lamp gave much more light than was required for a reading lamp, but who cared? Cliff did not want to waste any more of his drinking time on a piddling reading lamp.

Anna Lee Cole spent most of her conscious life indulging her gambling habit. She probably gambled in her dreams. She belonged to several poker clubs on the Internet. She and her friends found a way to gamble for money using the computer and the World Wide Web. Once every year, a gambling casino in Las Vegas offered free rooms in their luxurious hotel if you gambled for eight hours in their casino. Cliff and Anna would take advantage of the offer each year. Anna was an experienced gambler; she never won big, but she never lost big, either. Her winnings were just enough to keep her playing the game and hoping to win big.

When Cliff and Anna went on their annual gambling safari to Las Vegas, they would leave Lisa and Roger home alone. Roger spent a lot of time in the kitchen, preparing the family meals and cleaning up. A large pass-through window connected the kitchen and the dining room. Roger could serve the prepared food through this window with little effort. The dining room and living area amounted to one large, open space. There was approximately thirty-six feet between the pass-through window and the back of the living area, where Cliff's chair and reading lamp are located.

Cliff and Anna Lee left for their gambling safari early one Friday morning in December. Although Cliff did not enjoy gambling, he did appreciate the free drinks that came as a gift from the casino. At the casino, Anna Lee would feed the slot machines, and Cliff would position himself to be in the path of the cocktail server on her path through the gamblers. Overall, both Cliff and Anna Lee satisfied their individual cravings at the casino.

Meanwhile, back at the Cole home, Lisa Marie had just taken her shower and put on a very thin silk nightgown. She sat at the dining-room table, writing an entry in her diary. Roger was in the kitchen, cleaning up from the evening meal. Cliff had forgotten to turn off his reading lamp before he left for Las Vegas, and it was still on. Lisa was between Roger and the powerful 300-watt lamp.

Lisa had never had the trinkets and dolls most little girls just take for granted. She had found a discarded rag doll in the trash that she cherished. That rag doll was the only doll in her life. She never had nice clothes like the other little girls in her classroom at school. She never had a store-bought new dress or shoes. All of her apparel came from the Goodwill secondhand store. She never had money to buy ice cream and candy like the other girls. All the spare money in the Cole household went to satisfy Anna Lee's gambling habit. Lisa had been denied the simple joys of just being a beautiful little girl.

Roger was very industrious and full of energy. In addition to performing his many chores at home, he was able to hold down a night job at a fast-food restaurant. Roger had saved his money and bought a custom French racing bicycle. He paid just under $3,000 for the bike and then added another $800 in accessories. The bike was the envy of the neighborhood; everyone admired Roger's racing bicycle. Roger always kept the bike chained to the front mailbox post while he was at home. Lisa would just sit on the front porch and gaze at the bike and wish she could ride it, but Roger never let Lisa ride his prized bike. Lisa was known in the neighborhood as the girl who had the brother with the bike. The racing bike was very lightweight. Roger liked to show off by holding the bike with one hand at arm's length.

Off and on, Roger had had several girlfriends. None of the girlfriends lasted very long. As rumor had it, as soon as he scored with a girl, he dropped her and found another.

Lisa sat at the dining-room table, composing her diary entry. She would sit up straight and rear back in her chair and place both hands behind her head while she recollected memories for her writing. She would then lean forward and write a few more sentences in the book.

Roger peered through the pass-through window at Lisa as he dried the clean glasses with a kitchen towel. He could see the outline of her beautiful virgin breast through her thin silk nightgown. His casual glances turned into a constant stare.

After wiping all of the clean glasses, Roger put the towel down, left the kitchen, and sat down at the table next to Lisa. Roger positioned himself so that Lisa was between him and the powerful reading light. He was able to get a close-up view of the pointed nipples on her cone-shaped breasts. The more he stared at her breasts, the more excited he became.

Roger asked Lisa if she liked his bike.

Lisa said, "Everybody likes your bike."

Roger said, "What would you say if I gave it to you?"

"You are joking. You would never part with that bike."

"I'm thinking about getting a Volkswagen Beetle," Roger explained. "I've saved up over $3,000, and the manager at the fast-food restaurant has agreed to put the rest of the money. He said that he would take the payments out of my paycheck. I'll tell you what: if you let me play with your tits for an hour, I'll give you the bike."

Lisa said, "Are you sure?"

"I'm sure."

"You won't hurt me?"

"No, I won't hurt you."

Lisa asked, "You promise?"

"I promise. What do you say?" Roger put the keys to the bicycle padlock on the dining-room table.

Lisa responded in a very low, quivery voice, "Okay."

Roger walked around behind her and cupped his hands around her warm, soft breasts. Roger suggested that they go lie down. He asked her to remove her nightgown, and she did.

They went into Lisa's bedroom, and she lay on her back. Roger lay on top of Lisa and began to suck her breasts. Roger was very excited from watching Lisa from the kitchen pass-through window. It took only a few minutes before Roger reached down and grabbed Lisa's panties and began to pull on them forcibly.

Lisa raised her buttocks up slightly off the bed to keep Roger from tearing her panties. Roger immediately penetrated her.

Lisa began to cry. "Stop, Roger! You're hurting me! This is not part of the deal. Please stop. I do not want this. Stop, Roger! Please stop!" Lisa sobbed harder.

Roger ejaculated in her within seconds. Roger got up from the bed, leaving Lisa to cry and sob. Roger went into the dining room and retrieved the bike keys from the table. He returned to Lisa's bedroom and tossed the bike keys upon the bed, saying, "It's yours." Lisa seized the keys and held them in a death grip as she continued to weep.

After about an hour, Lisa got up, showered, and put on a red wool sweater and blue jeans, still clutching the keys to her new bicycle. She went to the mailbox post and unlocked the padlock that secured the bike. She mounted the bike and started the downhill ride away from the Cole home.

Near the bottom of the hill, Lisa and her bike were doing over forty miles per hour. Her long, blonde hair streamed straight back from her head. The cool Arizona wind whistled in her ears. She felt great. In fact, she never in her whole life had had such a feeling of freedom and joy.

Lisa was too tired to pedal back up the hill, so she walked the bike back home. She would stop every so often and just admire her new bike. The keys were still clutched in her left hand.

Lisa and Roger never had much to do with each other after this horrible incident.

Lisa's Seventeenth Birthday

During lunch break at school one day, the girls were sharing stories of their experiences on their seventeenth birthdays. One of the girls went on a camping trip with her family. She was able to take a boat ride around the lake in southern Utah. She showed everyone the photos of the beautiful scenery around the lake stored on her cell phone. Another one of the girls told of her trip to the Adirondacks Mountains in upper New York State. She also had photos of the Finger Lakes in New York. A third girl told of her trip to Europe. She had photos of the Eiffel Tower and the Arc d'Triomphe in Paris, France. She also had photos of the old ruins in Greece.

All of the talk of beautiful scenery and wonderful times built up anxiety in Lisa. She was looking forward to her seventeenth birthday with great expectations.

Anna bought a generic, premade, seven-inch cake for Lisa's seventeenth birthday. Roger was able to fashion a cone from some old parchment paper he found in a discarded kitchen cabinet. Roger cut a small hole on the small end of the cone and filled the cone with a sugar and butter mixture. He was able to write Lisa's name on the cake just before he left the house to go to work.

After Roger finished his artwork on the cake, Anna placed seventeen candles on the cake that she had found in the attic. On the next day, December 2, Anna brought the cake into the dining room with all seventeen candles ablaze. It took three puffs before Lisa could extinguish all seventeen candles.

Anna asked Cliff to carve the cake. Cliff carved a super large piece and said, "This one is for the birthday girl." He balanced the slice of cake on a regular kitchen knife. As he approached Lisa's plate, the cake slipped off and landed on the table.

Embarrassed, Cliff backed away and then stumbled forward, toward the table. He put his left hand out to help stop his forward motion, but his hand went right into the cake. His hand smeared the cake and icing all over the tabletop. Anna got a dirty, but damp, dishcloth from the kitchen and wiped off Cliff's arm and hand.

Anna gave the dirty dishcloth to Lisa and said, "Here, you clean up this mess—my Manhattan Poker Club will be on the Internet in two minutes, and I feel lucky."

Lisa wiped the icing and cake crumbs into a makeshift cardboard dustpan. Tears came to her eyes as she cleaned the top of the lacquered cherry tabletop. A tear rolled down her cheek and onto the table she had just cleaned. She stared into the teardrop, and she could see a beautiful little blonde girl. The girl was in a room full of people all laughing and singing. The girl was surrounded with boxes, packing material, wrapping paper, and several red wool sweaters.

Her friends would come up to the little girl and give her a gift, saying, "Happy birthday, Lisa." As she gave the table one final sweep with the dirty kitchen washcloth, her teardrop went away, along with her dream.

The Bright Yellow Volkswagen Beetle

It was exactly one year to the day from the time that Cliff and Anna Lee Cole had taken their last annual gambling trip to Las Vegas, that they were on their way again. They left early in the morning to take advantage of the casino's deal on a free room in the luxury hotel. Anna carried a little canvas bag full of quarters for her marriage to the slot machines. Cliff carried a thermos full of his favorite drink. Again, they left Lisa and Roger home alone.

After Roger had prepared lunch for himself and Lisa, and they had consumed the meal, Roger came and sat down at the dining-room table next to Lisa.

Roger said, "Do you remember last year when you let me suck your tits?"

"Yeah, and that's not all you did," Lisa responded.

"I'm sorry for that. I just got carried away. Your tits are the greatest that I have ever seen."

"Cut it out, Roger—I don't want to hear that kind of talk," Lisa bounced back. "Roger! Don't you have a girlfriend?"

"Yes," Roger admitted, "I've gone out with Susan down at the fast-food restaurant a couple of times. She's twenty years old and kind of chubby. We neck in her car in the driveway after work sometimes. There is a driveway all around her house. Just to the left of the house is a driveway entrance from the street. It goes all the way around the house and ends at a tall, thick hedge. On the other side of the hedge are the sidewalk and then the street. There is a streetlight on a tall pole at the end of the driveway on the street side of the hedge. Sometimes, the streetlight is not burning. The kids on the street like to shoot their slingshots at it. A boy was arrested last year for shooting a .22-caliber rifle at the light.

"Anyhow," Roger continued, "Susan and I were parked in her car, with the bright light shining in our faces. It was two thirty in the morning, and no one was around. We were in the backseat of her car, and she pulled her dress up past her hips, and I lay on my back with the back of my head on her bare leg. I reached up and unhooked the front snap on her bra. When

I lifted up her sagging breasts, I could see lots of tiny, red pimples, and some of them were open and oozing clear, sticky goo. I said to her, 'Just think, I had these in my mouth last night.'"

Lisa said, "Come on, Roger. Quit talking like that—I don't want to hear it."

Roger said, "You know, most of the girls I go out with have tits that sag down on their bellies. Yours stick straight out, with no sag at all."

"Roger, stop it!"

"Okay," Roger responded. "Lisa! Do you like my bright yellow Volkswagen Beetle?"

"Yes, I like your yellow Volkswagen Beetle. Why do you ask?"

"What if I gave it to you?"

"Quit your joking, Roger."

Roger said, "I am going into the army next week, and a new recruit is not allowed to have a car on base. The car is paid for, and I have thought about selling it. I'll tell you what I'll do: I'll give it to you if you give me a blow job."

"Come on, Roger. You wouldn't give it to me, and besides, I don't know how to do that."

"I gave you the bicycle, didn't I?"

"Yeah."

"All you have to do is suck me down here," said Roger.

"Oh, that sounds filthy!" Lisa exclaimed.

"I'll take a shower and make sure it's good and clean. What do you say?"

"Well, give me the keys."

"I'll put them here on the dining-room table," Roger said, "and you can have them when we're through."

"You promise not to hurt me?"

"I promise."

Lisa had wanted to ride in the yellow Beetle for a year.

"Okay," Lisa said. "I'll do it."

They went into Lisa's bedroom after Roger showered, and Roger removed his trousers and lay on Lisa's bed. Lisa had a difficult time finding a comfortable position to perform the required task.

Lisa received several instructions from her brother. Just as Roger was about to reach his climax, he grabbed Lisa's hair near each ear and pulled her down upon himself. This action caused Lisa to gag. Then she vomited all over Roger.

Roger got up and said, "Damn, Lisa, you puked all over me!"

Lisa said, "Okay, now give me the keys."

"Hell, no! You puked all over me—I'm not about to give you the keys!"

"If you don't, I'm going to report you," Lisa threatened.

"Go ahead and report me. I'm going into the army next week." Roger took another shower, put his clothes on, and went to his job at the fast-food restaurant.

Lisa straightened her clothes, got on her bicycle, and rode to the police station. She told the police sergeant all about what happened. The police picked up Roger at his workplace and booked him for having sex with a minor. Roger was twenty, and Lisa was only seventeen. Because of Roger's dealings with the army recruiter, and because he was deemed likely to flee, the bail was set at one million dollars.

Two days later, when Cliff and Anna Lee returned from their trip to Las Vegas, Lisa really caught hell.

Anna's words were, "How could you do this to your brother?"

Cliff said, "Who's going to do the work around here?"

Anna said, "I cannot believe you would do this. Well, I guess you are going to learn how to cook."

"And clean the house," Cliff added.

Anna said, "Well, young lady, you sure got us into a mess."

"But Mom, I was raped."

Anna asked, "Why couldn't you just keep it quiet, Lisa?"

Not one bit of pity or sympathy for Lisa existed in the Cole household. Lisa had just been raped, but all of the concern in the house was for Roger and the loss of his services.

Three weeks later, the court decided to send Roger to prison for six and a half years. The Child Protective Agency asked the court to remove Lisa from the Cole home. The court ruled that the Cole home was not a fit place to raise a seventeen-year-old girl, and that she should be placed in a foster home until her eighteenth birthday. The court assigned Lisa to Cora's Foster Home, a home approved for girls eight through eighteen years old. Three other girls lived in the home: Dorothy, Cora's daughter; and Beth and Barb Collins.

The Cora Pitts Foster Home for Girls

Lisa had been in the foster home less than a week when the three other girls decided that Lisa needed to be initiated. Dorothy grabbed Lisa and threw her on the bed. Dorothy held Lisa's arms and Beth held Lisa's legs while Barb penetrated her with the wooden handle of a mop.

Lisa began to cry and beg them to stop.

When they let her up, Dorothy said to Lisa, "Don't tell everybody that you are a virgin—you have just been had by a mop."

Lisa sat on the side of the bed, sobbing. Beth and Barb laughed until they cried. Dorothy said, "If you tell Cora, we all will deny it, and Cora will label you as the troublemaker you really are."

Cora's bedroom adjoined the girls' bedroom, with a door between. As one entered Cora's bedroom from the girls' bedroom, a wardrobe cabinet sat immediately to the left. On top of the wardrobe were five expensive, ceramic Hummel figurines.

Beth stepped inside Cora's bedroom and noticed the Hummels. She picked up one of a boy and girl kissing. She tossed it toward Barb, saying, "Guess what they are going to do next?"

The Hummel hit Barb's hand, but she dropped it. The ceramic Hummel broke into three pieces.

"Look what Lisa did!" Beth said.

"Yeah," Barb agreed, "Lisa broke Cora's Hummel."

All three girls said in three-part harmony, "Lisa did it."

Per her license and contract agreement with the state, Cora Pitts was to furnish food and shelter for the girls assigned to her. An auditor from the state would inspect the Cora Pitts Foster Home once a year for contract conformity. The state supplied clothing, medical care, and dental care for the girls. Once a month, the state welfare agency would give each girl a stapled brown paper bag containing soap, a washcloth, and a box of sanitary napkins in it. In addition, a church group would give each girl a personal kit each month that contained a bar of soap, toothpaste, a fingernail file, and a box of sanitary napkins. The state-furnished sanitary napkins were the old-fashioned, soft, absorbent, external type. The ones furnished by the church group were the insertable type. Lisa did not like the newer insertable type and would swap with one of the other girls for the soft, absorbent external napkins.

A railroad spur ran behind the Cora Pitts Foster Home. The railroad people would call it a long spur. The purpose of the long spur was to make up the freight train for the cross-country trip. The rail switchyard was about a quarter mile down the track. The coal-fired switch engine would pick up the railcars from the short spur, as required by the shipping manifest. The switch engine would place the railcar onto the long spur to make up the train. There were thirteen short spurs in the switchyard to hold the railcars that were waiting for a train to take them to their destination. The switch engine's attachment of a freight car to the main train was always accompanied by a very hard jolt, as the latch required significant force. When the switch engine started out for the day, the coal tender just behind the engine was loaded with all the coal that the tender could hold. The sudden jolt caused some coal to fall off the coal pile on the tender.

Cora Pitts and the four girls would strike out every Friday morning to retrieve the fallen coal. Beth and Barb would carry one bucket, while Lisa and Dorothy would carry another bucket. While the girls were gathering the coal, Cora would look for wild collard greens. Cora used the coal to fire the cast-iron cookstove in her kitchen. The cookstove was actually an old wood-burning stove, but Cora liked the high heat from burning coal much better than wood. One of the stove's legs had been broken off. The stove was propped up with a piece of an old two-by-four and one red brick.

Even so, the stove was fairly level, as was evidenced by Cora's wonderful corn-bread cakes. Cora would bake the corn bread in two ten-inch-diameter cast-iron skillets. She would pour the batter into the skillets to a depth of one-half inch to three quarters of an inch. The cornbread would come out as a thin cake with a golden-brown crust on both sides. Cora would not allow the corn-bread cake to be cut with a knife; the girls had to break their servings off with their hands. They could use a knife to separate the crusts in order to insert a generous amount of butter. After the collard greens had disappeared from the serving dish, the girls would place a piece of corn bread on their plates and pour the rest of the juice from the collard greens serving dish into the corn bread. This last bit of juice was called "pot liquor."

The appealing taste of Cora's corn bread was exceeded only by the taste of her morning biscuits. Cora made her biscuits from scratch. She did not have a biscuit cutter. She fashioned each biscuit by hand; they were not perfectly round and did not have a nice dome-shaped top. The biscuits were irregular, to say the least—but good, however! Good they were. Once a week, Cora would serve the girls biscuits and gravy. She made her gravy from sautéed pork sausage that was broken into very small pieces. Cora would take a freshly baked biscuit, break it in half, put it on a plate, and then spoon on two tablespoons of the pork sausage-gravy. Mmmm, good—the girls just loved it.

One Saturday evening, during supper time, Cora leaned back in her straight-back dining chair and said, "Girls, what do you say that we have a real treat tomorrow for breakfast?" All eyes were glued upon Cora, and all ears were tuned to Cora's next words. Cora said, "Let's have homemade pancakes tomorrow for breakfast."

A joyous roar came from the girls as they heard those words. Cora said, "Tell you what. You girls go to the store and purchase one pound of pork lard, five pounds of all-purpose flour, one pound of butter, one quart of sweet milk, and some table syrup." Cora gave a crisp twenty-dollar bill to Dorothy and said, "Be careful with the change."

The girls wiped their faces with a napkin, and off they went to the grocery store. Beth and Barb took a shopping cart and went down one aisle while Dorothy went down another aisle and Lisa went down a third aisle, each looking for a particular item on Cora's shopping list.

Beth spotted some syrup and picked up a bottle. She read the label to Barb. She said that it was 100 percent A-grade, light amber, pure maple syrup. She asked Barb, "How's this?"

Barb said, "Most syrup is made from sugar water with a little maple syrup added for flavor. Let's give the pure maple a try."

Dorothy and Lisa found the rest of the items on the shopping list. When the girls got home, Cora began to unpack the shopping bag and place the items on the proper shelf in the pantry.

When she got to the syrup, she exclaimed, "What the hell is this?" Then she looked at the store receipt and again exclaimed, "Eight dollars! Have you girls gone mad? I can't afford eight dollars for a bottle of table syrup!" She fumbled angrily with the plastic seal on the bottle cap.

Dorothy said, "Well, that is what Lisa picked out."

Cora said, "I should have known better than to send you to the store, Lisa." Finally, she got the thing open and tasted the syrup. She smacked her lips and said, "You know, this is pretty damn good."

Preacher Pepkins and Cora Pitts

A few weeks after Lisa arrived at the Cora Pitts Foster Home, she found herself alone with Cora. Lisa had noticed the bad disfigurement on Cora's right cheek, and wanted to ask Cora about it in order to satisfy her curiosity.

Lisa approached Cora and said, "I don't want to sound nosy, but I am curious about the scars on your right cheek. There seems to be a large chunk of your cheek missing. If you don't want to talk about it, that's okay. I am just curious."

Cora said, "Well, it happened about six years ago, while my husband was still alive. However, let me back up and tell you a little about Preacher Pepkins—that's the man who shot me. Have a seat, Lisa, and I'll tell you the whole story."

Cora Pitts, her husband, and her daughter, Dorothy, had lived in a small mining town east of Phoenix, Arizona. When the demand for copper was high, the copper-mining company built thirty-six houses to attract sufficient employees for the mines and the processing plant. During the peak production period, the mine had 3,200 employees. The company houses were built on three city blocks. All of the houses faced north, and each house was exactly alike. The mining company got a good price break from the building contractor, as he could use cheap labor if the building project was simple. These houses were known as "shotgun houses." If you opened the front and back doors of the house, you could see straight through the house. Each house had three windows on each side. All of the windows in each house lined up with the windows in the neighboring house.

When the demand for domestic copper evaporated, the mining company began to buy foreign copper for their processing plant. The foreign copper had so many impurities that it would not run in the copper wire extruders. The mining company built a small plant to remove the impurities from the foreign copper. The new plant only needed less than two hundred employees. The mining company closed the copper mine and auctioned off the company houses. The real-estate company in New

York who bought the houses in turn rented them out and sold them to new homeowners.

Cora Pitts and her husband had lived in one of these houses. Their house was the third house from the end of the street. The two houses west of the Pitts's house were vacant. A preacher and his wife purchased the house immediately to the east of the Pitts house. A young, single man named Samuel Kolinsky rented the next house farther to the east. When Samuel moved in, he had a live-in girlfriend. She had money and supported Samuel Kolinsky for about two years. She caught him cheating on her, and she moved out.

Preacher Pepkins did not have a church of his own. He was a freelance preacher. He filled in when a regular preacher was sick or on vacation. Preacher Carlyle had a church in Leveen Valley. Preacher Carlyle was a laid-back type of preacher. His sermons were very well organized; he would spend many hours preparing each sermon.

The church members in Leveen Valley collected money for three years to pay the way for their preacher to go to Israel and visit the birthplace of Christ. The Leveen Valley church deacons contacted Preacher Pepkins for an appointment to fill in for their preacher while he was on the trip to Israel.

The regular Sunday evening church service starts at 7:00 PM and lasts for three hours. On the first Sunday of Preacher Pepkins's job at the Leveen Valley Church, he arrived a little early to "test the water out," as he put it. It was a normally a forty-five-minute drive from his home to the Leveen Valley Church, but Preacher Pepkins left home at 5:45 PM.

Preacher Pepkins and his wife always retired early. Therefore, as soon as he left home, Rose Ann Pepkins took her shower and prepared for bed. She always paraded around the house in her night robe. The robe had no buttons or zippers, though it had once had a cloth belt. However, the belt had been lost years ago. She liked to stand by the open window, adjust the robe, and wrap it tightly around her five-foot-six, 130-pound body just to tease Sam.

Sam, the next-door neighbor, liked to watch the show from his open window. This evening, Rose Ann opened the robe wide open and moved her hips in a circular motion for Sam's pleasure. Sam signaled for her to drop the robe, and she did. Rose then signaled for Sam to come over, and he did. There was no chance of being caught; as Preacher Pepkins would not come home until well after 11:00 PM.

Preacher Pepkins began his sermon promptly at 7:00 PM. It took him only a few minutes for him to begin walking from one end of the podium to the other, waving his arms, crying and screaming, and preaching his "hellfire and damnation" sermon. About ten minutes into the sermon, he left the podium, went down into the auditorium, pointed his finger at one of the women in the front row, and said right to her face, "You are going straight to hell if you don't repent!"

This woman so happened to be the wife of the head deacon, who was at the back of the church, counting the money from the collection offering.

The head usher and his helper immediately rushed to the podium and seized Preacher Pepkins. With each man grabbing an arm, they escorted Preacher Pepkins out the door; Preacher Josh Pepkins's sermon had only lasted twelve minutes, and he was on his way back home.

When the preacher got home, he opened the unlocked front door and went into the house. The front door had not been locked for about six years. The spring that held back the latch was broken, and the door lock was inoperative. He noticed that the bedroom door was shut, which was a little uncommon in the preacher's home, as he and his wife both liked the ventilation that the open door gave. When he opened the bedroom door, he was shocked to see his wife lying on top of a male figure.

The preacher immediately turned and rushed to the walk-in pantry at the other end of the house. There he retrieved his loaded .16-gauge, full-choke shotgun. By the time the preacher returned to the bedroom with his shotgun, the neighbor had put his trousers on and fled the house.

His wife had put on her night robe. The preacher stood in the doorway, raised the gun to his hip, and fired at his wife. The preacher and his wife were approximately five feet apart, and the shotgun charge flew in a very tight pattern, missing her completely. The charge went over Rose Ann's shoulder, out the bedroom window, and into Cora's bedroom window.

The major part of the charge struck Cora on her right cheek. The charge tore out a large chunk of her cheek tissue. Two of the pellets struck Cora just under her right eye. Luckily, none of the pellets entered her eye.

Cora was rushed to the hospital, where the doctors performed emergency temporary procedures on her face. Cora did not have medical insurance, nor did she have the money for the proper cosmetic surgery. The operation left Cora permanently disfigured. She had a large, sunken-in place on her right cheek, and the skin was stretched under her right eye to close the wounds from the shotgun pellets. Her right eye was never completely closed.

Cora's husband was killed in an auto accident. He rear-ended an oil truck that had stopped on the freeway in a very bad dust storm. She received a small insurance settlement. She moved from the little mining town to a suburb of southern Phoenix, Arizona. There she obtained her license and established a foster home. Cora was always self-conscious of her facial disfigurement; she would never go to the grocery store to purchase food. She would always send her daughter, Dorothy, or one of the girls under her care in the home. The only time that she left the house was to pick collard greens along the railroad track or to pick up the fallen coal.

Beth, Barbara, and Rebecca Collins

When Beth and Barbara Collins were brought to the Cora Pitts Foster Home by the Child Protective Agency, the only explanation given to Cora was that the girls were from a dysfunctional home. The girls were to remain under the custody of a state-licensed foster caregiver until they reached the age of eighteen. Although Cora questioned the agency several times, no further information was given to Cora. Cora Pitts put on her detective hat and came up with the following story to satisfy her curiosity about the two Collins girls.

Leonardo Collins became suspicious when he observed many expensive clothes and other items around the house that he knew his janitor salary would not afford. He looked at the e-mail inbox on his wife's computer and discovered that his wife, Rebecca, had been acting as a call girl while he worked at his janitor job at the high school. He made a date with her under an assumed name on his computer. The deal was that they would meet at the Starbucks coffee shop and then go to a hotel, and he would give her $100. Leonardo went to the coffee shop at the appointed time. He went directly to Rebecca's table, slammed $100 on the table, and walked out.

As soon as he got home, he packed a small suitcase and headed for the Greyhound bus terminal. He bought a ticket to San Antonio, Texas, where some of his relatives lived. Rebecca and her two daughters continued to live in the small upstairs apartment on Van Bremen Street in downtown Phoenix, Arizona.

When he arrived in San Antonio, Leonardo telephoned the police and told them of his wife's activities. The police set up a sting operation to trap Rebecca and her johns. One of the undercover detectives solicited a known prostitution pimp to participate in the sting operation. The detective promised not to report him for a parole violation in exchange for his cooperation. The decoy pimp invited an unsuspecting john, and the three of them descended upon the Collinses' apartment. Rebecca poured each one a drink in the manner of a true professional. The drink, by the way was a Tom Collins.

The undercover detective had a hidden spy camera, and he photographed the real john fondling Rebecca's two young daughters. Rebecca was fully aware of what was going on.

Rebecca was arrested, and the Child Protective Agency took the two children away and placed them in a temporary state-run foster home. Later, the court ruled the Collins home was not a fit place to raise two underage girls; the court also ruled that both Beth and Barb Collins should be placed into a state-licensed foster home until they reached their eighteenth birthdays. Rebecca was placed on two years of probation for her cooperation in the prosecution of the child-fondling john. Barbara and Beth Collins wound up in Cora Lee Pitts's foster home.

The facility was in Cora's home itself. The house had two bedrooms and two bathrooms. Cora used the smaller bedroom with her own private bathroom; the girls enjoyed the larger bedroom with a shared bathroom. The girls were expected to keep their quarters clean as part of their duties.

Cora had an eighteen-year-old daughter, Dorothy, who lived in the large community bedroom. Dorothy Pitts was a slob. She always wore a man's white shirt, and it was usually dirty. In the front shirt pocket she had what she called her "snot rag." It was a filthy thing. Dorothy suffered from frequent post-nasal drip. Her left shirtsleeve was almost stiff from the wiping of her dripping nose on it. When Dorothy took a bath, her grime always left a ring on the bathtub. When the other girls called her attention to the ring, her comment was, "Well, it shouldn't bother you that much. I don't bathe that often." One of the girls mentioned the fact that Dorothy's white shirt was filthy dirty. Dorothy responded, "Well, I guess it is time to turn it inside out. You know, it is clean on the inside. I can get another two weeks' wear out of it that way before I have to wash it."

Phillip Thompson

Phillip Thompson was an amateur musician. He would play and sing anytime he found someone to listen. He played at all of the local jam sessions in the area. He would invite other musicians over to his house to make music. He played guitar each Sunday during the music session at church.

Phillip obtained a government grant when he was 45 years old to build a combination fast-food facility and concert stage for local musicians to play on. The public was invited to come and listen to the free music. Phil would position his portable grill upwind from the audience and cook baby back ribs. The smoke and barbecue aroma would entice the audience to order food. The establishment did attract some big-name bands occasionally. For the most part, the musicians would play free or sometimes for a meal of ribs, if they would play music for four hours.

Phil had four servers. Two servers wore shorts and sold drinks only. The other two servers, who wore white trousers and low-cut, black blouses, sold food and drinks. An RV trailer parked next to the kitchen was used as a dressing room for the servers. The trailer had a washer and dryer installed. Phil had a rule that if the server's uniform became soiled in the smallest manner, the server must change to a fresh uniform. The washer and dryer were for that purpose. Phil kept a table and chair in the front of the trailer and used the setup as an office. The back bedroom remained in the original condition as purchased. Sometimes Phil would spend the night in the RV, if he had had a rough day and was too tired to drive home. Occasionally Phil would discover a suspicious character casing out the supply shed. He would spend the night on the premises with his .44-caliber, ten-inch Ruger handgun.

Phil needed a replacement server for one who had just quit. He placed an ad in the local newspaper for an experienced server. Lisa noticed the ad in a discarded newspaper the day after it came out. She thought about applying for the position, but Cora would probably put the kibosh on that. After all, she was under a court order to stay in the foster home under

Cora's guidance. She finally decided, *What the heck? It is worth a try.* She rode her bicycle to Phil's place.

With her striking beauty, Lisa got the job, no questions asked. She dreaded the confrontation with Cora, but much to her surprise; Cora went along with the idea.

Cora said, "This is highly irregular and may be a bit illegal, but you can contribute a little toward the expenses around here, and we all will keep it quiet … as long as you are here when the state inspector makes his annual inspection."

Lisa was received well by the other servers, except for one. The troublemaker server held a conference with the other girls, and she pointed out the city ordinance that forbids underage girls from selling alcoholic beverages. This was brought to Phil's attention. Phil ruled that the three older girls would take orders and collect the money from the customers. Lisa would deliver the food order to the customers. This plan worked well, and everybody seemed to be happy.

One Friday evening, Phil was in the RV trailer, going over the books at the office table. Lisa came in and asked if she could launder some of her street clothes in the washer and dryer. Phil replied that it would be okay.

While the clothes were being laundered, Lisa asked Phil if he used the bed in the back of the trailer. Phil answered that he slept there sometimes, on rare occasions.

Phil said, "Why do you ask?"

"The place I am staying at is a living hell! Cora's daughter, Dorothy, is real mean to me. She hurts me every chance she gets. Beth and Barb are always playing tricks on me. Beth took my underwear and tossed it up into a tree. Barb took my only brassiere and hid it in Cora's kitchen garbage can. The next day, around noon, Barb felt that she had gotten all the fun out of the joke that she needed, so she said, 'I know where your bra is.' We went into the kitchen and looked into the garbage can, but the garbage can was empty. Cora had emptied the kitchen garbage can into the dumpster outside. The dumpster was picked up at ten o'clock and emptied into the landfill.

"Beth took my cotton nightgown and put it into Cora's kitchen oven cookstove," Lisa continued. "When Cora built a fire in the cookstove, my nightgown went up in smoke!"

Phil told Lisa that she could sleep in the bed in the back of the trailer.

"However, you know that I have to sleep here also upon occasion," he added.

Lisa said, "That's okay. You are a perfect gentleman here in the daytime, and I know that you will be at night."

Phil replied, "I guess you are right—I don't want to wind up in prison with your brother, Roger. I am sure we can find a workable solution to this problem, right?"

Dressing-Room Trailer

Lisa slept alone in the RV trailer for three straight nights. On the fourth night, Phil told Lisa that three very suspicious characters had been casing out the non-perishable food shed. He had seen these people lurking around before, and one of them had fondled the padlock on the side door.

Phil said, "I think these guys will come back later on tonight, after we close. I am going to be ready for them. You know that we both will occupy the bed in the back, don't you?"

"Yes, I know," Lisa answered. "That was the deal, right?"

Phil waited for Lisa to retire before he went to bed. Lisa had on her silk nightgown, and she was between the sheets with a light blanket over her. Phil slept in all of his clothes on his side of the bed on top of the covers; he wanted to be ready in case he heard a suspicious noise.

Phil got up in the middle of the night and made a search of the grounds, but he did not see anything out of place.

Two nights passed before Phil again told Lisa that he would be sleeping in the RV trailer. Lisa responded, "Well, it's your trailer."

"Are you sure that it doesn't bother you?"

"No," Lisa responded.

This time, Phil suggested that they keep the top sheet between them. Lisa had on her silk nightgown with a sheet and light blanket over her. Phil removed all of his clothes except his shorts. He slept on top of the top sheet and pulled the light blanket over him. Both Phil and Lisa got a good night's sleep.

A week passed before they slept together again. Lisa told Phil, "It must be very uncomfortable sleeping on top of the sheet. It will be okay if you want to sleep under the top sheet."

"Thank you. Yes … I think I'll take you up on that." That night, both slept together under the top sheet, with only occasional, innocent, temporary touching during the night.

A month later, they slept together again. This time, Phil said to Lisa, "I think some pajamas would be more comfortable than that nightgown."

Lisa said, "Yeah, this nightgown is a little awkward at times."

"Tomorrow, we'll go and get you a nice pair of pj's."

Again, the two got a good night's sleep.

The next day, Phil and Lisa picked out two pair of women's pajamas at J.C. Penney. The next two nights, Lisa tried out her new pajamas, wearing a different pair each night.

The next time that Phil and Lisa slept together, Lisa wore her new pajamas to bed. Phil asked Lisa if she liked to snuggle up. Lisa said that she had never snuggled up with anyone before, but she was willing to try it. Lisa lay on her right side, with her back toward Phil. Phil turned on his right side to face Lisa's back. He moved up close to Lisa, so that most of their bodies were touching through Lisa's new pajamas.

Phil said to Lisa, "How is that?"

"That feels good," Lisa answered.

"Great. Good night, Lisa."

"Good night, Phil."

The next night, Phil suggested to Lisa, "You know, you don't have to wear those new pajamas every night; I bet snuggling in the nude would feel great."

"Snuggling is all, right?" Lisa asked cautiously.

"Sure. Remember, you are just seventeen, and I don't want to wind up in prison with your brother."

"Okay, I'm game. Let's try it." They both got in the nude, except for Lisa's panties and Phil's shorts, and snuggled up close to each other. Neither spoke a word, and they drifted off to sleep in a night of bliss.

The next morning, Lisa said, "I want to thank you, Phil, for being a perfect gentleman last night. I was a little afraid that you might lose control of yourself and do something that we were not supposed to do. By the way, I really enjoyed last night."

Phil said, "That was the most wonderful night I have ever had. We must do it again."

The next night, Phil and Lisa cuddled up in the nude at bedtime. Lisa's back was toward Phil, and Phil pressed tightly against Lisa's back. He placed his left arm on top of Lisa's left arm, which was resting on top of her left side. He cupped his left hand around her shoulder.

Lisa reached up with her right hand, took hold of Phil's left hand, and placed it on her left breast. Phil gave her breast a gentle squeeze but then immediately removed his hand, saying, "I don't think the law will allow this, Lisa."

Phil woke up and got dressed at 5:00 AM. Lisa was still asleep. Phil went to the kitchen and fired up the grill. He cooked two eggs, sunny-side up. He cooked two slices of bacon until they were very crisp. He prepared a large bowl of fresh fruit. He buttered two slices of sourdough toast. A fresh cup of coffee with cream and sugar rounded out the meal.

He took the breakfast to the trailer on a large serving tray. Lisa was still asleep. Phil picked up his guitar and began to sing a lullaby. Lisa woke to the singing and guitar music.

"Good morning Lisa. Have you ever had breakfast in bed?"

"No."

"Well, you are going to now," Phil said as he placed the food tray on Lisa's stomach on top of the covers.

Lisa commented, "This is delicious, Phil. But what did I do to deserve this kind of treatment?"

"I guess you know that I think of you as more than just a friend, Lisa."

"Yes, I know."

"In fact, Lisa, I like you very much," Phil continued.

Lisa said, "Phil, can I tell you something?"

"You can tell me anything."

Lisa spoke slowly. "All the people that I know are out to hurt me, or take something from me, or do things that make me feel bad. Phil, you are the only person I know who has treated me like a human. I will always be grateful for you being in my life. You are the only person in the world I can trust."

"Lisa, whenever you are near, all of the light seems a little brighter. All of my troubles and worries just seem to vanish. I feel so good whenever you are around. You have a birthday coming up in a couple of months … December 2, I believe?"

"That's right. I will be eighteen."

"I'd like to do something special for you on your eighteenth birthday," Phil said. "Have you ever been on a cruise?"

"You mean, like on a boat?"

"A big boat, Lisa," replied Phil. "If you are on the bottom deck and you get on the elevator, you can go up for fourteen floors. There are three outside swimming pools and one that is inside. There are two mealtime dining halls, one anytime dining hall, and a twenty-four-hour buffet. Two big theaters put on Broadway plays. There is a tennis court and a complete spa where you can get a great massage. There is always some kind of entertainment going on. Oh, and yes, there is a fabulous gambling casino."

Lisa said, "That sounds great!"

"We don't have much time to lose," Phil said. "We must apply for your passport, and that takes over a month. We have to go shopping for some evening clothes; you must be dressed up for the captain's ball. Just in case people get curious about the difference in our ages, I will dress you up as a nurse, and you can pretend to be my personal nurse ... so we need to buy a couple of nurse's uniforms. I will book a short cruise first and if you like that we will take a seven day cruise. If everything goes ok we will take a cruise around the world."

First Cruise: Cancun

Lisa did not have any problem getting her passport; Anna Lee knew right where her birth certificate was located. Lisa and Phil went on a grand shopping spree. They bought two black brassieres; black leggings; two black blouses; three white blouses; a low-cut, red evening dress; and a black, low-cut evening dress. They purchased a three-piece dress suit. Two pairs of high-heeled shoes rounded out the uptown shopping spree. At the nearby mall, they found two one-piece swimsuits and one two-piece swimsuit. Three pair of shorts and three tank tops finished the mall shopping. On the way home, they stopped and bought two pair of tennis shoes, two pair of white jeans, and one pair of blue jeans. They also stopped by a medical supply house and purchased two white nurse's uniforms.

Phil said, "We'll have to go back to the mall; I forgot the little red suitcase."

Phil told Lisa that the cruise ship was very safe, but there was always danger involved in floating out in the middle of the ocean.

"We should take out an insurance policy, in case there is an accident, and one of us survives," Phil said.

"Phil, that is gross."

"Yes, I know, Lisa, but there is always a small chance that something may happen. I want you to have a good life if something should happen to me. I talked to my insurance broker already, and he said that we would have to take a physical exam before we got the policy. Tomorrow we will go to my family doctor and get the physicals, okay?"

Phil and Lisa arrived at the doctor's office as soon as it opened, at 9:00 AM. They were the only ones in the waiting room. Lisa immediately picked up a couple of magazines from the side table. She began to thumb through the *Lady's Journal*, licking her index finger to provide moisture to turn the pages easily.

Phil, noticing Lisa's action, immediately took the magazine from her and said, "Lisa, don't ever handle magazines in a doctor's waiting room. Mostly sick people come here, and they handle the same magazines. They, too, will lick their index fingers to turn the pages, as you just did. I just read in the news that one person in every thousand has HIV. One in every 800 has the gonorrhea bug. It is unknown how many people have genital herpes, as most cases go unreported.

"Most of these magazines are here for a month until the next issue comes out," Phil continued. "Each magazine is handled hundreds of times. When you lick your index finger to turn the page, you place your wet finger on the same spot that several people have placed their wet finger. I can almost guarantee you that somewhere in that stack of magazines, HIV is lurking. During the flu season, people are coughing and sneezing all over the magazines. The magazines are just full of influenza bugs. So Lisa, it is best that you do not touch the magazines in the waiting room."

Lisa responded, "Phil, I didn't know. I'll go wash my hands right now."

Phil and Lisa got a thorough checkup from the doctor, and everything checked out okay. Two days later, they received the certificate required by the insurance company. Phil booked a three-day cruise to Cancun, Mexico, for two. The New Poland cruise line said that the price of the three-day cruise would be subtracted from the fare for the world cruise.

They flew to Miami, Florida, and spent the night at a motel right next to the seaport. They boarded the ship at 10:00 AM. Phil had a great time showing Lisa around the ship. He made an appointment for Lisa to have a massage in the ship's spa. Phil explained the difference between the three dining halls. Lisa decided that they would try one of the closed-seating restaurant. She said that it would be nice to have the same table and same waiters for each meal. Of course, they could always skip the appointed time at the closed-seating diner and go to the twenty-four-hour buffet. Phil agreed.

In Cancun, Mexico, they went ashore and had lunch at one of the local recommended restaurants. Phil told Lisa that the restaurant would not serve alcoholic beverages to a minor. However, he said that he would order a large margarita, and they could share it.

"Be sure to get two straws," Lisa told him.

This was the first time that Lisa had tasted an alcoholic drink. They had chile relleno for lunch and shared the margarita.

Halfway through the margarita, Lisa commented, "You know, this is damn good."

Phil commanded, "Better lay off the drink, Lisa. I've never heard you talk like this before."

"Phil, you are just a party pooper," Lisa retorted. She needed a little help getting back to the ship. Once in the stateroom, Lisa pretended to be more intoxicated than she really was. Phil helped her to get undressed, and she did nothing to help. Of course, Phil enjoyed every minute of it.

Lisa did not have a single mole, wart, or even a scar on her whole body.

Lisa said, "Stop staring, and put on my pajamas." Phil obeyed her.

The next morning, Phil and Lisa decided to go for a swim before breakfast. Lisa put on her two-piece swimsuit. She wrapped a large bath towel around her body and then took off for the swimming pool.

As Lisa unwrapped the towel from around her body, all eyes watched every move she made. Lisa was enjoying the attention she was receiving. Lisa could not swim, so Phil held out his arms for Lisa's support in the shallow water. She lay on Phil's arms and pretended to kick her legs, as if swimming.

Phil was full of excitement at having such a beautiful girl in his arms. Phil would look around to see the onlookers watching them. To be sure, they were watching Lisa, not Phil.

After about an hour, Phil and Lisa decided that they had had enough of the pool for the day. Lisa climbed out of the pool and wrapped the towel around her body. One man on the deck above leaned over so far to try to get a better look at the Lisa show that he fell over the railing. He was not hurt, as he landed on a stack of extra lounge-chair pads.

Phil and Lisa had breakfast in the twenty-four-hour buffet. They had thin slices of smoked salmon, fried eggs sunny-side up, crisp bacon, half of a grapefruit, a bowel of fresh papayas, sourdough toast, strawberry shortcake, and chocolate milk.

Lisa began to sop up the remaining egg yolk with a piece of sourdough toast.

"Lisa!" Phil exclaimed. "What are you doing?"

Lisa replied, "I'm sopping up the rest of my egg with this toast. Why?"

Phil said, "You can't do that on a cruise ship. People are watching you."

Lisa looked up and saw about twenty eyes glued upon her. Lisa said, "We do this all the time back in the foster home."

"You are not back in the foster home, Lisa. You are on a cruise ship, and that is just not acceptable etiquette here."

Lisa responded, "Okay, Phil, but I hate to see the good part of my egg go to waste."

"If you want more eggs, the waiter will bring you some."

Lisa said, "No, thanks. I'll just let the best part of my egg go down the drain."

After that, the waiter came around and insisted that Phil and Lisa have a cup of the restaurant's specialty coffee and of course a nice piece of Danish pastry.

Phil said to Lisa, "You are going to have to cut it out; you are going to ruin that beautiful body by eating too much."

After breakfast, Phil took Lisa to the ship's spa and signed her up for a full-body massage. Phil waited in the spa lobby until Lisa was finished with the massage. They walked through the gambling casino and observed large stacks of money on the gaming tables.

Alaskan crab legs were the specialty offering during the noon meal at their closed-seating diner. For dessert, they had raspberry crème brûlée. Lots of warm, hard, French bread was served during the meal. For sure, they had some of that special coffee. Little Danish cookies were served on the side. Phil had to ask Lisa not to dunk her cookie into her coffee; several people were watching the Lisa cookie-dunking show.

After the noon meal, Phil took Lisa on another tour of the ship. The billiards room had eight pool tables, all of the highest quality. Phil and Lisa tried their hand at pool, but neither was very good; they barely managed to keep all of the balls on the table. The next stop was the Internet café. They counted thirty-six computing stations, and a master printer was located next to the café supervisor. A scanner was also available. There was an extra charge for each of the services; none were covered by the passage fare.

Next, they tried out the tennis court. Each of the three tennis courts was staffed by a professional, certified instructor. Phil and Lisa were no better at tennis than billiards.

The next stop on Phil's tour was the exercise room. Lisa counted three treadmills, four stationary bicycles, several weight-lifting stations, numerous arm and leg exercisers, and a body-stretching station.

A trip through the gambling casino wrapped up the tour. Again, Lisa began to count the number of slot machines, poker tables, giant spinning wheels, and various card-gaming units.

Lisa commented to Phil, "My mother, Anna Lee, would go crazy in here—absolutely nuts!"

They were still feeling the large lunch and were not very hungry, so they decided to just have an ice-cream sundae and stop for the day. When they arrived at their stateroom, Phil sat down on an overstuffed straight chair that did not have any armrests. He signaled for Lisa to come sit down upon his lap. Lisa sat on Phil's lap with her right side facing Phil. Phil put his arms around Lisa's waist with his hands locked together on the other side of her. Lisa placed her right arm around Phil's neck and drew her face close to Phil's left ear.

"Phil, can I tell you something?"

"Sure, Lisa."

"I had a dream last night. In the dream, the ship docked at an isolated island, and the natives took over the ship. They took you and me to a hole in the ground that was about twenty feet around and ten feet deep. All around the outside rim of this hole were native men in grass skirts, and each one had a long pole with a sharp arrowhead on it. They were shifting their weight from one foot to the other. It was kind of like some sort of dance, but each one was doing his own thing. They weren't moving together in any real rhythm.

"After a while," Lisa continued, "some of the natives brought a rope ladder to the pit. The ladder was made from two ropes with sticks tied to the ropes to make steps. The natives unrolled the ladder down into the pit. A native with a tall hat on climbed down the ladder and walked over to us. He seemed to be some kind of leader or ruler or something. He had a cup of white liquid in his hand, and he drew a white line across the bottom of the pit we were in. He then said to us, 'One of you will die; the other one will live. You must choose among yourselves which one will die. The one that you choose to die must step across this white line; the other one must stay on your side of the line."

Lisa paused. "I stepped across the line," she whispered. "Phil, you never mentioned the word 'love' in any of our talks about our relationship, and neither have I. Maybe I just do not know what love is. Phil, if this dream situation should occur in real life, I would step across the line. Phil, if it weren't for you, I don't know what I would do." Lisa's voice broke up as she uttered these words.

Phil's eyes filled with water, and big tears rolled down his cheeks. Lisa leaned forward and let her lips shortly touch Phil's lips, and then she got up, took her shower, and prepared for bed.

Phil continued to sit in the overstuffed chair and just stared at the wall as big tears rolled down his cheeks. The front of his shirt became soaking wet from his teardrops.

First Cruise: On the Way Back Home

Dusk had fallen and the ship was halfway between Cancun, Mexico, and Miami, Florida, on its return leg back home when Phil summoned Lisa to come look out at the ocean from the stern of the ship. He suggested that Lisa lean over the rear railing to see the giant propellers as the ship rode the ocean waves. The propellers were about six feet long, making the total diameter of the propulsion system about twelve feet. Phil told Lisa that the propellers on the speedboats on the lake turned very fast, but the ones on this ship turned very slowly. Lisa was able to see the propellers pretty well.

Phil called Lisa's attention to the white wake the ship left behind. She said, "That is beautiful."

In turn, Lisa called Phil's attention to the little lights in the wake. Phil told her that the lights were phosphorous crystals. He said that normally, the crystals lay on the bottom of the ocean, but when something disturbed them, they floated up to the surface. The disturbing force imparted some unwanted energy into the crystals, and the crystals gave up this energy in the form of visible light.

After about half an hour of watching the ocean from the stern of the ship, Lisa said, "Phil, I don't feel good. I think I am going to throw up."

"Okay, Lisa, we will go to the ship's infirmary and see if they can give you something to help you."

Back in the stateroom, Phil commented, "Lisa, I took you to the stern of the ship for a purpose. When we take the world cruise, it would be nice to have a balcony stateroom where you could see the ocean all the time. However, if you are prone to getting seasick, that would not be such a bright idea. Being seasick is not a very pleasant situation. So it looks like we will have to take an inside cabin for the long trip."

Lisa took the medicine that the nurse gave her at the infirmary. After about an hour, she was back to normal.

They decided to skip the evening meal and just stay in the room. Phil ordered two strawberry daiquiris from the room-service phone. Lisa enjoyed her drink.

After a while, Phil spoke. "Lisa, last night, you seemed to question why I never use the word 'love' when referring to our relationship. First, we need to define what we mean when we say 'I love you.' If it means physical desire ... well, there is plenty of that. Does it mean a desire to make the other one happy? Well, I qualify there also. Last night, you said in so many words that you would die for me ... is that part of love? How about a desire to be together forever ... is that love? The good feeling that surrounds me when you are around ... is that love? Lisa, I love my cat; I love country music; I love to paint and carve wood; I love to travel. Lisa, I cannot say that I love you in a world where these other loves exist that have just diluted the meaning of the word. 'Love' does not properly describe my feelings for you. Maybe if I could speak Latin, I could find the proper words to express my feelings for you, but hell, I flunked Latin in high school. I wish I could find words powerful enough to express my true feelings toward you.

"I know that there is a great difference in our ages," Phil continued, "and this makes it more difficult to express myself and not sound phony."

Lisa interjected, "I am sorry if the difference in our ages troubles you. I promise you, Phil, it does not matter to me at all. I do not have the problem with the word 'love' that you do. So I am going to say it: Phil, I love you very much; I love you from the bottom of my heart."

"Lisa, last night, you said some things to me that tore at my heart. It is said that grown men are not supposed to cry. I just could not find the proper words to tell you how much I really love you. And the tears just kept coming."

Lisa said, "You are the sweetest man in this whole wide world."

Phil asked, "Would you like to sit on my lap again?"

"Sure." This time, she leaned forward and placed a passionate kiss on Phil's lips. She backed away and looked into Phil's eyes, and then leaned forward and kissed him repeatedly.

Finally, Phil said, "Better stop it, Lisa. You are building a fire that might get out of control if you keep it up."

Lisa said, "Yeah, you're right—I'm only seventeen."

Before the ship docked at the Miami pier, Phil booked passage for two on a ship called the *Flying Goose*, which would leave Los Angeles, California, on December 1. This was a seven-day cruise to Vallarta, Mexico, by way of the Baja peninsula and back. The *Flying Goose* was about one and one half times bigger than the ship they were on. Since Phil booked the Baja cruise on the high seas, the New Poland Cruise Line gave him a 20-percent discount. The cruise line also reminded Phil that the entire cost of the Baja cruise would be deducted from the world-cruise fare.

The ship docked at Miami, Florida, at 8:00 AM on November 29. Phil and Lisa flew from Miami to Los Angeles that same day, which made them early for the Baja cruise.

Phil wanted to show Lisa where the movie stars lived. They rented a car at the air terminal and took a grand tour of Hollywood. They visited the movie studios and some of the shooting sites.

That evening, after supper, Lisa sat down on the side of the bed next to Phil.

"Can I ask you a question?" she said.

"Shoot."

Lisa commenced by saying, "Last night, you gave me a lot of mumbo jumbo about why you could not tell me that you loved me. Then you turned around and told me that you love me very much. Phil, I do not understand you. If you really love me, why don't you kiss me or touch me? Are my breasts not good enough for you? Do you really like me?"

"It's not right for a forty-five-year-old man to kiss and fondle a seventeen-year-old minor," Phil said. "To condemn me for not touching your breasts is not fair. How many times at night have I admired your perfectly shaped long legs in my dreams? How many times at night have I felt your legs wrapped around me? How many times in my dreams have I kissed you passionately? How many times in my dreams have I felt your little hard nipples between my lips? How many times have I dreamed of burying my face between your tits?"

After a moment of silence, and Lisa spoke. "Phil, I'm sorry. I should have never doubted you. Come on, eighteen—come on and get here!"

Phil said, "When you turn eighteen, one of the first things that I am going to do is to kiss you all over. I am going to unleash all of the passion that I have for you. No holds barred."

Second Cruise: Day One

It was 10:00 AM on December 1 when Phil and Lisa boarded the *Flying Goose* for their seven-day Baja cruise. They had booked an inside cabin because of the possibility of Lisa getting seasick. Their cabin was on the first deck, on the very bottom of the ship. Upon opening the entrance door to the cabin from the passageway, Lisa found herself in a little hallway next to an open closet. She could not use the closet space until she closed the entrance door facing the closet, and to the left was a hanger rod with twenty coat hangers. Just to the right of the hanger rack was a set of shelves for clothing storage. The shelf that was at eye level contained a safe for valuable-item storage. Between the hanger area and the main room was the shower and toilet area. This also had its own door. A folding door divided the closet area and the main stateroom.

Phil and Lisa's room was just four doors from the bow or front of the ship. Upon leaving the stateroom and passing three other rooms on each side of the aisle, they wound up in a very small lobby area serviced by the only elevator at the front of the ship. This elevator went all the way up to the fourteenth deck and had an operating door in the front and the back. When this elevator was going up, Lisa would eventually notice, it always stopped on the seventh deck. Six more elevators serviced the fifth deck through the fourteenth deck. In addition, two glass-enclosed observation elevators serviced decks five through nine, which were connected by an enclosed atrium. This area was used for the champagne-glass-stacking show. The twenty- four-hour buffet was on the bow of the ship, on the fourteenth deck. The lobby in front of the twenty-four-hour buffet was quite large, as it must house the six main elevators and the two entrances to the buffet. Although the single small elevator's front door opened on the seventh deck, only its rear door opened on the fourteenth deck. This rear door opened onto the outside deck area. At the right and left of the elevator were two cranes with lifeboats ready for launching. On the way to the buffet, Lisa and Phil passed between the enclosed lobby area and the lifeboats. They encountered a three-sided cubbyhole before reaching the lobby door. Inside the cubbyhole was the ship's laundry chute. This laundry chute went from the fourteenth deck all the way down to the first deck. The laundry-chute cubbyhole had no dedicated illumination; the string of lights hanging from mast to mast provided sufficient illumination.

After wandering quickly around the ship, Phil and Lisa returned to their stateroom to finish unpacking. They decided to try the closed-seating dining room for lunch. Their table was next to the main service aisle. They were assisted by a very pleasant waiter, along with two young women who served coffee and other drinks. Lisa tried on some of her new clothes for the noon meal. She looked gorgeous.

Across the main aisle from Phil and Lisa were four young men at a table with no female companions. One of the men had on a brown pin-striped suit. Phil noticed that the man kept glancing at Lisa. Phil did not assign much significance to it, as Lisa was something great to look at.

Phil and Lisa agreed to try the twenty-four-hour buffet for the evening meal. The twenty-four-hour buffet had two sections. The starboard side remained open when the port side changed from the breakfast menu to the lunch menu. The starboard side closed again when the menu changed from lunch to dinner. The port side was open while the starboard side made the menu changes.

After lunch, Lisa put on her one-piece swimsuit. She had fun in the pool while Phil relaxed in a reclining chair. Phil dozed off for about a half hour, and when he woke up, he noticed the gentleman in the brown pin-striped suit leaning over the guardrail on the deck above, with his eyes glued on Lisa in the pool.

Back in the room, Phil reminded Lisa that his love for her depended upon her loyalty to him. He said, "If you are ever unfaithful, you must take your little red suitcase and go; I cannot love anyone who is not faithful."

"Phil, you don't have anything to worry about. I'm yours—all yours."

Phil and Lisa took a longer, more leisurely tour of the ship before supper. They noticed a full-sized four-lane bowling alley, but decided to try it out later. They looked at the tennis courts, but remembering their last cruise, they decided to pass that up also. They walked by the spa, and Phil signed Lisa up for a massage. They looked at the two large theaters, but no shows were being presented at that time.

At one of the small theaters, Phil signed Lisa up for a Karaoke contest.

"Phil, I can't sing," Lisa complained.

"Well, the rest of the contestants probably can't sing, either."

As they approached the twenty-four-hour buffet, they noticed a stairway going up to a nightclub. A chain across the entrance displayed a sign that read, "Open at midnight."

Phil said, "We'll have to check that out."

Phil and Lisa took a quick pass through the buffet to get a feel for the offerings. So many different kinds of food were available that the choice was perplexing. They both decided on the prime rib, but Phil wanted his rare, and Lisa chose well done.

Phil said, "You like your roast burned."

Lisa responded, "You like your roast still on the hoof."

Creamed potatoes, gravy, and a side of green beans rounded out the main course. Again, a gigantic decision had to be made at the dessert bay. There must have been a hundred different desserts on display. They both finally decided on raspberry crème brûlée.

After they had enjoyed all they could eat, Phil suggested they go to the room and rest, as they had a full day the next day.

As they got to their stateroom, Lisa said sarcastically, "What's doing tomorrow?"

"You just wait and see."

"Oh, yeah," Lisa said. "It's somebody's birthday."

Phil responded, "I wonder who?"

Lisa came over and sat on the side of the bed next to Phil. Phil put his arms around Lisa and said, "I guess one little kiss before tomorrow won't hurt."

"I've been waiting for this for a long time, Phil."

They hugged and kissed each other with great passion.

"We better stop," Phil said, "or we will spoil things for tomorrow."

"Yeah, tomorrow, you can show me how much you really do love me, right?"

"You got that right, sister."

With those words, they each showered separately and prepared for bed. Lisa was first to reach the bed and exclaimed, "Hey, Phil, there is chocolate candy here on my pillow."

Phil explained that this was one of the little ways the cruise line showed their appreciation for having them aboard."

Lisa said, "Well, I have already brushed my teeth, so I'll just have it tomorrow."

"Whatever turns you on," Phil responded.

Lisa just laughed

Second Cruise: Day Two

Very early, at about five in the morning, Phil woke up all full of vinegar. He began to sing as Lisa slept: "Happy birthday to you, happy birthday to you, happy birthday my dear love, Lisa, happy birthday to you!"

Lisa opened her eyes and spoke. "Oh, how sweet of you, Phil."

Phil demanded, "Lisa, take those pajamas off. You know I promised the day you turned eighteen, I would kiss you all over your lovely body. Well, you are eighteen now, so here goes!"

Lisa wasted no time in removing all of her sleeping attire. Phil ever so gently slid over on top of Lisa and placed a passionate kiss upon her waiting lips. Her cheeks and neck were next. Phil nibbled on each earlobe. As he slid down the bed, he finally arrived at her breasts. Her little nipples found their way between Phil's lips.

"Oh, Phil, I love you!" Lisa exclaimed.

Phil continued down her body, kissing and nibbling, until he reached her toes. A trip back up her lovely body to her waiting lips completed the journey.

"Did you enjoy it?" he asked.

"Did I ever!"

"You know, I think we ought to have sex," Phil said.

"Well, it's about time."

Later, Phil suggested that they shower together: "I'll wash your back, and you can wash mine."

"That's a deal."

Phil said, "In my dreams, I shampooed your long, blonde hair several times. Would you let me shampoo your hair?"

"Sure," agreed Lisa.

Once in the shower, and with the water adjusted to a nice, warm stream, Phil wrapped his arms around Lisa and held her very close to his body. After several passionate kisses, they had sex under the running stream of warm water.

Exhausted, they climbed into the bed after drying each other with a large bath towel. They slept until 10:00 AM with their arms entwined around each other. After another shower, they were on their way in a search for food. It was too late for the regular closed-seating diner. They made their way to the twenty-four-hour buffet. Again: decisions, decisions! Scrambled eggs, bacon, hash browns, and coffee seemed to fit the bill.

After the very late breakfast, they decided to try out the bowling alley. They were not too bad at bowling, except for Lisa's first ball. It seemed that she had forgotten to let go. Lisa, ball and all, went sliding down the alley.

The alley manager came over and said, "Folks, that's not the way we do it around here."

Lisa responded, "Well, that's the way we do it in West Virginia." Lisa had never been to West Virginia.

Unbelievably, they found some bicycles and a riding track. The rental price of the bicycles was not included in the cruise fare. Phil had to put the cost on his *Flying Goose* credit card. At least they were good at riding bicycles.

The tennis courts were next. Although there were nets all around the courts, Lisa was able to put two tennis balls into the Pacific Ocean. Oh, yes, the cruise line applied an extra charge for the two balls.

They discovered a miniature golf game. Of course, they had to try that out.

"You deserve a medal," Phil told Lisa. "Not one golf ball went into the water this time!"

"Oh, go jump in the ocean yourself," Lisa said.

After a strenuous afternoon, they arrived at the closed-seating diner in time for the evening meal. The special offering for the night was Alaskan giant king crab legs served with melted butter and fresh lemon slices. Lisa had never had crab legs before; this was a real treat for her.

Phil and Lisa had their regular reserved table next to the service aisle. Lo and behold, right across the service aisle was the man in the brown pin-striped suit. This time he was all alone.

Phil held his menu up to his face, as if reading. He watched the man peer at his menu, at Lisa, and then back to his menu. Lisa was aware of the attention she was receiving and was obviously enjoying it. Phil did not show any awareness of the flirtation between Lisa and the man in the brown pin-striped suit. Phil fixed his eyes on a corner across the aisle, and when he quickly brought his gaze back to Lisa, she was looking across the aisle at the man in the brown pin-striped suit. Phil did not say a word to Lisa at dinner.

Later, at a dance, Phil once again told Lisa that if she ever cheated on him, she would not be the girl he was in love with: "If you cannot be faithful to me, you should pack your suitcase and leave."

Lisa said, "Why are you saying these things to me, Phil? I love you. I will always love you. You scare me, talking like that!"

Phil said, "I just want to make sure you know how I feel."

At the dance, several men asked Lisa to dance with them. Lisa always asked Phil for permission. Lisa was not a very good dancer, but on a slow dance, if her partner held her very tight, she could follow okay. One of the men danced with Lisa and when the dance was over, he escorted her back to Phil's table. He graciously said to Phil, "Thank you, sir. You have a lovely daughter."

Phil and Lisa danced three times to some very slow music. Phil did not mind at all as he held her lovely form next to his body.

Back at their room, Phil gave Lisa some basic dance lessons. Lisa said that she wished she could dance the jitterbug like some of the girls she had seen at the dance.

Phil said, "Well, that's easy. All you have to do is shift your weight from right to left and back to your right in a 'one, two, three' count. Then you do the same thing starting on your left foot. Now your right foot is free, and you back step, like this." Phil gave a quick demonstration. "While you are doing what I just showed you, I am doing the same thing, only on the other foot." They tried it, and then Phil said, "This is the basic step. Now you can add under-arm and over-arm turns to make it look good."

Lisa said, "No, no, that is enough for tonight."

"Oh, come on, Lisa, while we are at it, let me show you another dance step very similar to the one you just learned. This one has a 'one, two, three' count also. They were doing the waltz, remember? Well, it is a much simpler dance than the jitterbug."

Phil put his arms around Lisa, and they did the steps.

"I guess you know that when we are dancing on the floor, I cannot hold you this close," Phil said.

Lisa said, "yes, I know."

Phil suggested that they make a trip to the ice-cream bar and bring an ice-cream sundae back to the room.

Lisa said, "I'm game for that."

She chose a strawberry sundae, and Phil got a chocolate one. They very carefully transported the sundaes to the first deck and home. Phil suggested to Lisa that she should remove her evening clothes so that they would not be soiled for the next dance.

"What do you want me to put on?" she asked him.

"Your birthday suit will be fine."

"I don't understand."

"The suit you had on when you were born," Phil explained.

"You mean nothing?" Lisa asked.

"You catch on quick," Phil said.

Lisa disrobed and sat on the side of the bed with Phil. She took a bite of her sundae and then offered Phil a bite.

"Come a little closer, Lisa."

Phil took a spoonful of the chocolate syrup from his sundae and smeared it on Lisa's breast. He said, "You know it looks a lot better there than on the ice cream." He leaned over and licked the chocolate from her breast and commented, "And it tastes a lot better, too."

"Phil, you are a pig!"

"Oink, oink," Phil answered. He pushed Lisa down on the bed, so she was on her back. He then painted both of her breasts with the chocolate syrup before licking them clean.

After the sundaes were consumed, they showered together and went to bed.

Second Cruise: Day Three, Cabo San Lucas

On the third day of the voyage, the ship docked at Cabo San Lucas, Mexico, at eight in the morning. No tugboats guided the mammoth ship to the dock; the captain pulled the ship alongside the dock and brought it to a complete stop. Lo and behold, the ship started to move sideways, toward the dock. As it approached the dock, its speed dropped almost to zero. The big ship barely kissed the dock, with no jolt at all.

Due to some customs regulation, the crew would not let the passengers off the ship until 10:00 AM.

Phil and Lisa had breakfast in the closed-seating diner. In addition, guess who was across the aisle from them? Yep, the man in the brown pin-striped suit. Phil had become accustomed to the man's constant stare.

The food was great, and the service superb. After breakfast, they walked all around deck seven.

When ten o'clock arrived, Phil and Lisa went ashore. Cabo San Lucas is famous for its quality tequila. Phil told Lisa, "We must get some of that good tequila before we return to the ship."

They decided to have lunch at one of the local Mexican restaurants. They scoured the beachfront cafés, looking for a nice, clean-looking place to eat. They could have hired a taxi, but they chose to walk and absorb the local atmosphere. They must have walked five miles and considered several restaurants before they found the ideal restaurant. Meanwhile, Lisa saw several little trinkets that she took a fancy to, and Phil purchased them for her.

After lunch and another five miles or more of walking, they headed for the ship, as it was to depart at 6:00 PM. Phil and Lisa had to show their passports to get back on ship. Lisa had a hard time finding hers among all the stuff she had purchased. They came on board just in time for the evening meal in the closed-seating diner. They were still full from the Mexican venture, but they decided to try the evening's special anyway. They only ate a small portion of the serving and skipped the dessert completely.

It was about 7:30 PM when they got back to the stateroom. Phil plopped down in the easy chair and dozed off. Lisa watched TV for a while and then decided to get something to drink at the buffet.

Phil slept for about an hour before waking up to realize that Lisa was not in the room. He figured she was having a soda at the buffet. Phil put his shoes back on and headed for the buffet. He made his way to the single elevator and punched the button with "14" on it. When he got out of the elevator, he turned to his right and passed the lifeboats on his right side and the lobby on his left side.

As he approached the laundry-chute cubbyhole, he noticed a man standing in front of the laundry chute. As he drew nearer, Lisa, who was leaning against the sheet-metal casing around the laundry chute and in front of the male figure, spotted Phil's approach.

"Phil," she said. "I was just about to come and get you." She stepped away from the man in the brown pin-striped suit. "Let's get something to drink at the buffet," she suggested.

"Phil," Lisa said as the two of them headed to the buffet, "you have to meet John. It is so interesting to hear him talk. He has been around the world three times. He has been on twenty cruises. He was telling me about Hawaii—it sounds like such an amazing place! He is so fun to listen to. I want you to meet him. His name is John Cunningham. He has a balcony suite on the twelfth deck. Maybe we can get together sometime, huh, Phil?"

Phil responded, "Sure, Lisa. Sure."

Phil and Lisa got a hot chocolate in an insulated cup and proceeded to their room. Phil and Lisa did not exchange many words once in the room. They each showered and prepared for bed. They were both very tired from the long walk on shore.

Second Cruise: Day Four, Mazatlan

It took all night to sail from Cabo San Lucas to Mazatlan, Mexico. Phil and Lisa had breakfast in the twenty-four-hour buffet. While they were eating breakfast, an announcement came over the loudspeakers that the shore call would be at 10:00 AM. The final boarding call was set for 4:00 PM. It would take the ship about ten hours to travel from Mazatlan to Puerto Vallarta, as the ship could not travel at its full speed of twenty-four knots in prime fishing waters.

Phil bought Lisa a cheap digital camera. The memory card in the camera would hold about six thousand photographs. Lisa tried her best to utilize all six thousand storage slots; she snapped everything that was not moving. She took over two hundred photos of Phil, who posed with several nude female statues. Phil was not so happy when Lisa wanted to pose with a nude male figure.

Several old churches commanded a lot of attention from the ship's passengers. As Phil and Lisa passed a pub with a mariachi band playing inside, Phil detected the familiar scent of cigar smoke. Sure enough, the two of them sighted a brown pin-striped suit at the bar. They did an immediate about-face and walked away.

Phil and Lisa enjoyed the quaint Mexican shops. Most of the merchandise in the shops was fashioned for the tourist trade from the cruise ships. Nevertheless, Lisa was able to fill a shopping bag with items she just had to have.

She spotted an interesting little Mexican restaurant with lots of balloons and other hanging whirligigs drooping from the ceiling.

"I'd like to eat here," Lisa said.

"Why not?" Phil responded.

Each item on the menu had a side label: "mild," "medium," "hot," and "torture."

Lisa said, "I'm going to try a little bit of that torture."

Some of the menu items had Spanish names. This threw Lisa for a loop, but the waiter could speak fair English, and he was a big help. She finally chose a pulled-pork chimichanga covered with "torture"-grade enchilada sauce. The waiter suggested that Lisa have a side of sour cream to help with such a hot enchilada sauce. Phil ordered pork chili verde with the mild sauce. They shared a giant margarita.

The bread came wrapped in aluminum foil. Lisa burned her hand trying to unwrap the hot bread. When she finally got down to the bread, she exclaimed to Phil, "Look! The bread is thin and round."

Phil explained, "It's a Mexican tortilla—that's the way it's supposed to be."

Lisa sliced off a bite of her "torture"-grade chimichanga and put it into her mouth. She chomped down on the mixture and hollered, "Oh, my God! Phil! Please help!" She used her napkin to get rid of the food, but the fire remained. Phil told her to take a bite of the sour cream. This helped some. A swig of the margarita was even more help.

Lisa scraped all of the sauce off the chimichanga that she could. She said, "You know, this is very good once you get past the fire."

"Mine is excellent," Phil said.

After they had consumed the major part of the meal, the waiter came around to see if they would like a dessert. He suggested fried ice cream.

"Fried ice cream?" Lisa repeated.

The waiter said, "Yes, we actually fry the ice cream in hot peanut oil."

Lisa said, "Well, I am going to have to see this!"

The waiter brought two ice-cream bars on Popsicle sticks covered with a thick chocolate covering. Lisa said, "Well, I've seen everything now."

Phil suggested that they head back to the ship, as they were about three miles from the dock: "The boat will sail at four o'clock whether we are on it or not."

"Well, I would just as soon stay here," Lisa said.

"Come on—gather up your packages, and let's get on the move."

They made it back to the ship in plenty of time.

A small coffee shop on the ship operated in the late evening. It had small tables and offered donuts and other pastries. It was only open from 8:00 PM until midnight. They had not tried this one before, so they decided to do so that evening.

Phil and Lisa got a cup of coffee and two Krispy Kreme donuts each. At the next table sat an elderly woman with her coffee and donuts. She had diamond rings on each finger. Some of the diamonds were as big as Lisa's thumbnail. Lisa noticed that the woman picked up her donut with her little pinkie stuck straight out from the rest of her fingers and broke the donut into two pieces. She then dunked her donut half into her coffee.

Lisa gave Phil a swift kick under the table on his shins and said, "Look, Phil, she is dunking her donut—why can't I?"

"Go ahead and dunk your donut," Phil said.

Lisa stuck her little pinkies straight out, broke her donut in half, and then stuck one half into her coffee. She said, "I guess it's okay to dunk your donut if you stick your pinkies out like this." Phil just laughed. The woman next to Phil and Lisa heard the remarks that Lisa had just made. She smiled at Lisa and then continued with her dunking.

Phil suggested that they have a late supper in the twenty-four-hour buffet, as they had eaten a big meal at the Mazatlan restaurant, and it would be a while before they got hungry.

Back at the room, Phil said, "Let's call room service and order two strawberry daiquiris."

"I'll go for that," Lisa said.

"Lisa, Why don't you put on something more comfortable?"

"Let me see what I can find," Lisa responded.

She removed all of her clothes except for her panties and then wrapped a bathrobe around her body. She came back out of the bathroom and said to Phil, "How's this?"

"You look great," Phil said. He took off his street shoes and slipped on a pair of house shoes. Not much time passed before the bellhop brought the daiquiris to room 104. Phil stretched out in the recliner; Lisa sat on the side of the bed.

After about half of Lisa's daiquiri disappeared, Lisa came over and sat on Phil's lap. She said, "You know, I'm still feeling that margarita from back at the restaurant, and now this ... I'm about ready to boogie."

Phil opened her robe, peered inside, and said, "You look like you are ready to boogie." Phil asked Lisa if she was hungry.

"No, let's go to bed," she answered. In the bed, they hugged each other and then fell sound asleep.

Second Cruise: Day 5, Puerto Vallarta

The ship docked at Puerto Vallarta at six in the morning. The passengers were not permitted to leave the ship until 8:00 AM. At breakfast in the twenty-four-hour buffet, the voice on the public-address system announced that the ship would leave promptly at 4:00 PM. All passengers should be on board by 3:00 PM. Phil and Lisa left the ship at about 9:00 AM.

Lisa was amazed at the wonderful sand sculptures along the beachfront. Her camera got a good workout on the sculptures.

"Look at that hill," Phil said. "I don't think that we want to walk up that one. Let's get a taxi." At the bottom of the hill was a general-purpose store. The taxi driver said that this store had a little bit of everything for sale. The streets were very narrow, as the streets were built for a horse and wagon, not an automobile. The vendors along the beach said that some interesting sights awaited Phil and Lisa up on top.

The taxi driver did not make much haste going up the hill. He let Phil and Lisa off at the top to do some looking and photographing. The taxi driver waited for them to return to the cab. Again, Lisa photographed everything in sight.

The taxicab ride on the way down the hill was something else. The road was winding and narrow. As the driver approached an intersection, he would blow his horn without applying the brakes. Phil gritted his teeth and held onto the backrest on the seat in front until his fingers turned blue. Lisa just shut her eyes. As they wound through the curves, Lisa would wind up against the left-hand door and then in Phil's lap again. About halfway down, the driver asked if they would like to be dropped off anyplace in particular.

Sarcastically, Phil said, "Yes, I'd like to go to that little general store at the foot of the hill. I need some toilet paper."

"Phil," Lisa said, "you are a pig."

At the foot of the hill, near the general store, the driver let Phil and Lisa out of the cab. Phil paid the driver and thanked him for the safe ride back home. Phil and Lisa agreed that their unnerving descent had been the last of the taxi rides in Puerto Vallarta.

"Phil, let's just walk from now on."

"I gotcha," Phil said.

There were many statues and other interesting things to see in Puerto Vallarta. Phil and Lisa must have walked six or seven miles before heading for the ship's dock. All of the passengers made it back to the ship by 3:00 PM, as requested. The ship left the dock promptly at 4:00 PM. After about a half hour, the captain announced that the night's formal dance would be the last one on this cruise. The dance will start at 7:00 PM, preceded by a dance lesson by a professional instructor starting at 6:30 PM. The dress attire would be formal.

Phil and Lisa grabbed a quick snack at the twenty-four-hour buffet, took a shower, and began to dress for the dance. Phil was in the main stateroom and Lisa in the closet area.

Lisa said in distress, "Phil, I have a problem. My bra strap shows. The straps on this dress are skinny, and I can't hide my bra straps. We should have bought a strapless one!"

Phil said, "Well, take your bra off."

"I guess that a bra is to push them up," Lisa mused. "I don't need to push mine up—they're already pushed up!"

Lisa came out of the closet area and posed for Phil. She had on the $300 jet-black, low-cut evening dress, black hose, black high-heeled shoes, and a black pearl necklace around her neck. Her pure white skin framed in the black attire was like a picture from a fashion magazine.

Phil just stared at Lisa and said, "You look good enough to eat."

Phil and Lisa were early for the dance lesson. They were able to get a table right up against the dance floor. The dance lesson was for the waltz. The instructor explained that the basic movement in the waltz is the box step. He described the many variations to the basic box step; in fact, he encouraged them to make up their own variation. Lisa caught on to the waltz with ease. The instructor said that they could just dance the box step all night if they wanted to.

Lisa was quite pleased with herself, knowing she could dance all night long just doing the box step.

After the dance lesson was over, Phil and Lisa sat down at their ringside table and ordered a drink each. Just as the seven-piece band started to play, guess who appeared at the table in front of Lisa? Yep: it was the man in the brown pin-striped suit.

Lisa asked, "Do you care if I dance with John?"

"No, go right ahead, and have fun."

Phil could get a glimpse of the couple every now and then between the many dancers on the floor. They were a little too close to each other to suit him. When they rotated around the dance floor in front of him they separated somewhat. However, Phil noticed that John made an occasional glance down the front of Lisa's dress.

When that dance piece was over, John brought Lisa back to the table and said to Lisa, "Thank you for a very lovely dance." He then nodded toward Phil and left.

Lisa asked, "Did you know that we are going to be very close to Cabo San Lucas on the way back home? But we're not going to stop this time. Oh, and this ship has 2,800 passengers on it. Did you know the ship weighs 120,000 tons, and it can travel at twenty-four knots? That's about thirty miles per hour."

"Boy," Phil said, "you are just full of information."

"John told me," Lisa said.

"There's one thing I know: you smell like old cigar smoke. You are going to have to shower when we get back."

Phil and Lisa enjoyed the next five dances together. Thirsty from all the dancing, they sat down and ordered another drink each. It was not long before another man came over to the table and asked Phil if he could dance with the young woman.

Phil said, "Better ask her."

Lisa accepted his invitation, and they danced in a normal fashion. Phil and Lisa danced two more times together. Then, as the dance was about to conclude, the man in the brown pin-striped suit came over one more time.

This time, he asked Phil for permission to ask Lisa for a dance.

"Ask her," Phil said.

Lisa responded before the invitation was offered: "I'd be glad to."

Phil kept an eye on the two as they danced together. John would hold Lisa very close to his body, and then he would back off and peer down the front of her dress. Phil was glad when the dance was over, and he hurried Lisa back to the room.

It was about 10:00 PM when Phil said, "Lisa, I am exhausted, but I sure would like to have a hot chocolate."

Lisa said, "Why don't I change clothes and go to the buffet and get us both one?"

She removed the black evening dress and hung it up on its hanger. Next, her high-heeled shoes and hose came off. She put on her bra, a pair of blue jeans, and a pair of sneakers. As she buttoned up one of Phil's white shirts, she said, "I'll be back in a few."

Phil did not hear her leave, as he dozed off as soon as he hit the chair. It was about 10:00 PM when Phil woke up, and Lisa was still not in the room. He decided to go to the buffet and get the hot chocolate himself; maybe he could meet Lisa there and share it with her. He put on his old sneakers and headed for the single elevator. After entering the elevator, he punched the button for deck fourteen.

When the elevator reached deck fourteen, Phil stepped out, turned to his right until he met the lifeboats, and then turned to his left. He followed the row of lifeboats on his right side, with the lobby on his left side, until he saw a man standing in the laundry-chute cubbyhole.

As he approached the cubbyhole, he could see Lisa's head over the man's shoulders. She was looking up toward the ceiling but with her eyes closed. She was leaning against the sheet-metal casing around the laundry chute.

The man in the brown pin-striped suit was bent toward Lisa's chest. As Phil got closer, the man sensed Phil's presence and backed away from Lisa. Phil could see that Lisa's shirt was unbuttoned all the way down to her belt, and her bra was pushed up over the top of her breasts.

When the man backed away from Lisa, she brought her head back to the normal position, and she recognized Phil standing there. She immediately pulled her shirt together to hide her exposed breasts.

Phil looked straight into her eyes and said, "Don't bother to come back to the room."

He turned away and made quick time to the elevator, which was still waiting on the fourteenth deck.

As he walked away, he heard Lisa say to John, "Let's go to your room—I will make you very happy."

Phil did not hear John's response. What John said was, "We can't go to my room—my wife is there in her wheelchair."

"Please tell me you are joking!" Lisa said.

"I'm sorry, Lisa. I am a married man, and my wife is in a wheelchair in the suite."

"Oh God, no!" Lisa said. "What am I going to do?" She quickly pulled her bra down over her breasts and buttoned all twelve buttons on Phil's white shirt. She hurried to the elevator. The elevator was still on the first deck. Slowly, the numbers lit up one after another, pausing on seven for what seemed to be an eternity. Finally, the elevator finally reached deck fourteen.

In the meantime, Phil rushed to the room on deck one and packed Lisa's street clothes into the little red suitcase. He set the suitcase outside in the passageway. He locked the door and applied the deadbolt and the safety chain. He then sat down and began to weep.

When Lisa arrived on deck one, she ran to Phil's room and knocked on the door. Phil did not answer.

"Phil, I know you're in there. Please let me in. I know that you are hurt, and I want to make it up to you. Phil, I have nowhere to go."

"Go to John Cunningham's room," Phil said.

"I can't. He's a married man, and his wife is in the room."

"I'm sorry," Phil said.

"Phil, I have nowhere to go—please have mercy! I made a mistake, an awful mistake, and I am sorry. Please give me another chance. I will never, ever do anything like that again. Please, Phil, please! For God's sake, Phil, please let me in!" She began to pound on the door with both fists. "I know I made a mistake, an awful mistake. I will do anything to make it up to you—anything, Phil, anything," she cried. "I made a bad mistake. I don't know why I did it. John is a fast talker ... and a smooth talker. He is very convincing. I guess I was under his spell, and I was very weak. I wasted everything for a little thrill. Phil, you know I did not even get a thrill out of it. I hate myself for what I did. Please let me in! Have a heart, Phil."

Phil came to the door so that Lisa could hear and said, "I don't have a heart; you ripped it right out of my chest. I feel so empty. I am just a shell. I could never love you again."

"I don't know why," Lisa said, "but I gave my breast to John, and I was wrong. Phil, if you could take me back, and if you wanted me to, I would cut my breasts off and throw them into the Pacific Ocean. I mean it, Phil—I would do anything!

"I know that I hurt you," she continued. "I hurt you very badly. You were the only person in this world who treated me like a human. You were so kind to me. I hurt the person that I love ... I destroyed it all. I hate myself for hurting you, Phil. You were so good to me." She sat on the floor of the passageway and began to sob.

The neighbor directly across the passageway cracked open her door and peered at Lisa sitting on the floor in front of Phil's room. The neighbor next door, toward the stern of the ship, opened her door as well, and both she and her husband looked at Lisa.

"Poor girl," they said, and shut their door.

In one final attempt to get Phil to let her in, Lisa kicked the door several times and begged for forgiveness. Her voice was getting hoarse from the crying and begging.

"Please, Phil," she begged, "doesn't our love mean anything to you?"

"You are not the girl that I fell in love with," Phil responded. "Goodbye."

A dead silence fell over the hallway.

The neighbor directly across the passageway again opened her door, but Lisa and the little red suitcase were gone. The other neighbors, toward the stern of the ship, also opened their door. They saw nothing: no Lisa, no little red suitcase.

At 10:30 PM, a little Vietnamese man was leaning on the guardrail at the stern of the ship, watching the white wake trailing behind the ship. The string of lights running from mast to mast cast enough light on the water to make the phosphorus crystals do a native dance. As the Vietnamese man stood intrigued with the wake-water show, he suddenly noticed a bunch of blonde hair in the water.

A woman appeared in the water, waving her arms as if to signal for help.

The Vietnamese man hollered, "Lady in water! Wave arm! Lots of blonde hair!"

No one was around to hear him, so he turned and picked up the red emergency phone. A ship's purser answered the phone.

The little man said, "Lady in water. Lots of hair. Lady wave arm."

The purser said, "Let me get this straight: you see a lady in the water waving her arms. Is that right?"

"Yes," the little Vietnamese man said. "That right. Lady wave arm, want help."

"Hold on a minute—I'll get the captain." When the purser came back on the phone, he said, "The captain wants to make sure that it was a lady you saw in the water."

"Yes! Lady in water! Wave arms, and lots of hair!"

Two minutes elapsed before the captain announced on the public-address system, "Attention, ladies and gentlemen. It has been reported that a person may be overboard and in the water. We are going to turn around and search the proposed sighting area. We are traveling at the top speed of twenty-four knots. It will take about four minutes to gradually slow the ship to a complete stop. If we removed the power to the props all at once, everybody would be forced up against the forward walls. Once we have stopped, I will spin the ship around using the side thrusters. The first mate is taking care of the details of this operation as I speak. After we make the 180-degree turn, we will slow the ship to twelve knots. At that time, I would ask all the passengers to look for someone in the water, likely a woman with a massive amount of blonde hair. Thank you for your attention."

A good ten minutes had passed before the ship was heading toward the proposed area of sighting. The captain followed the whitewater wake that the ship had previously made, and eager observers lined the ship's side rails. In fact, John Cunningham had wheeled his wife, Rose, outside to help look.

The search began about twenty minutes from the time of the original sighting. At fourteen knots, the ship was about twelve miles away from the target area. Despite all of the onlooking eyes, no one saw any sign of a woman in the water. After a fifteen-mile run, the captain turned the ship around, and everyone on board searched the same path one more time—all without any results.

In the meantime, the first mate radioed the Coast Guard in Los Angeles and told them of the possible drowning. The Coast Guard dispatched a helicopter immediately. The Coast Guard helicopter arrived on the scene at about 3:30 AM. They were able to do a thorough search using their twin 30,000-candlepower searchlights.

Second Cruise: Day 6, the Detectives

At about 6:00 AM, a Coast Guard diver recovered the body of Lisa Cole. Rigor mortis had set in, and her stiffened right hand clutched a little red suitcase. The Coast Guard captain radioed the *Flying Goose* that they had the body of a female and needed to land on the *Flying Goose,* as they could not take her back to the United States. The nets and steel net stanchions on the three tennis courts were removed to make a landing pad for the Coast Guard helicopter.

When the helicopter landed on the *Flying Goose's* deck, it was met by the *Flying Goose's* medical team, and Lisa was pronounced dead by Dr. Susan Xiaokui Lee, the infirmary doctor. Lisa's body was wheeled away on a gurney to the infirmary walk-in cooler.

The Coast Guard radioed the Los Angeles Police Department that they had recovered a body of a female passenger from the *Flying Goose* from the water. Although the Los Angeles police had jurisdiction because the ship had sailed from the Los Angeles harbor, no detectives with current passports were available. The LAPD subcontracted the investigation out to the Lost Angels Police Department.

The Lost Angels police sent detectives Compton and Pulaski to investigate the case. The detectives were flown by helicopter from Los Angeles to the *Flying Goose* near Cabo San Lucas, Mexico; the tennis nets and support posts had already been removed to make a temporary landing field.

When the detectives descended from the helicopter, they made it known that a criminal investigation was under way and that they were in charge. They ordered the captain to drop anchor about twenty-five miles south of Cabo San Lucas, Mexico. The detectives began to apply yellow crime-scene tape all over the place.

The captain of the ship came up to Detective Compton and asked, "When do you expect to get this thing over?"

"I have no idea right now, Captain."

"You know, I have to have this ship back in LA within forty-eight hours."

"Well, Captain, I think you're going to be a little late," said Detective Compton.

The captain frowned. "You know that I am the captain of this ship, and I have a schedule to meet."

The detective was getting a little peeved at the captain and said, "Captain, I am in charge here, and there is yellow crime tape on the control-room door. Crossing crime-scene tape will get you a mandatory minimum $25,000 fine. You had better have your wallet wide open if you have any intention of moving this ship. Now, Captain, please stay out of my way."

After talking to the purser and getting all the information that they could from him, both detectives interviewed the little Vietnamese passenger.

Compton asked the Vietnamese man, "Did you see anybody push the girl into the water?"

"No, me no see lady push in water. I see woman wave left arm, lots of hair."

Compton asked, "Was anyone with you when you saw the lady in the water?"

"No, I see lady wave left arm. Lots of hair."

"I take it that you were alone on the back of the ship when you saw the lady in the water."

"Yes, I alone watch sparks in water."

Detective Compton told Detective Pulaski, "Talk to this John Cunningham fellow, and I will talk to this Phillip Thompson person."

Detective Pulaski had a little tape recorder to record all interviews. John and Rose Cunningham were very cooperative during the interview. The detective recorded every word of the interview. He took many notes as John and Rose spelled out their life story.

Detective Compton first talked to the neighbor directly across from Phil's room. They recalled the pounding on the door by a crying and sobbing Lisa. It seemed that the man in the room would not let her into the room.

Detective Compton asked, "Did you see or hear Phil enter or leave the room anytime after 10:00 PM?"

"No, sir," the man said, "we did not."

"Did you see the girl leave Phil Thompson's room, either alone or with someone?"

"We did not see the girl leave," the woman answered.

Compton asked, "Do you know if the girl entered the room during this confrontational period?"

"No, we don't know."

Detective Compton thanked them for their cooperation and said that he would probably be back. The detective then questioned Phillip Thompson.

He asked Phil, "Did or did you not push Lisa Cole off the ship and into the water?"

Phil began to cry, and a big lump swelled up in his throat as he answered in a very broken voice, "No. I loved that girl with all of my heart."

Compton said, "Yes, but did you push her overboard?"

"No, I did not," Phil replied.

"Did you leave this room between 10:00 PM and 11:00 PM?"

"No, I did not."

Compton commented, "I understand that you and Lisa had a little misunderstanding right after the dance. Do you want to tell me about it?'

Phil gave the detective the completely gruesome story. He concluded that in his opinion, it was John who had pushed Lisa overboard to keep his wife from knowing about his attentions toward Lisa.

Compton thanked Phil for his help and said, "I'll be back."

Detectives Compton and Pulaski met to compare notes in the eating area of the twenty-four-hour buffet. Little square tables lined the outside wall of the ship next to the glass observation area. Compton and Pulaski pushed two of the tables together and made a temporary office. They applied a generous amount of yellow crime-scene tape around their temporary office.

Detective Pulaski had two full cassettes in his little tape recorder and twelve pages of handwritten notes. Compton produced nine pages of notes. Compton started by giving Pulaski all of the details he gathered during his part of the investigation.

Detective Pulaski said, "I asked the Cunninghams to give me their life story, and I sure did get an earful. There is a lot of information here that is not pertinent to the case, but I let them ramble on, as something important may pop up. Well, here's what I got from both the recorder and my notes."

Second Cruise: The Cunninghams

John Cunningham was from a very poor family of sharecroppers who lived on a delta farm in Arkansas. Most of the time, the Cunninghams worked for a widowed woman who owned two 160-acre tracts of land. Rice was the main money crop.

The Cunninghams were never able to find the money to send John to college. John did graduate from high school. At nineteen, John got a job at a car dealership.

On his second day on the job, John met a customer with a flat tire, which John had his mechanics remove from the vehicle.

After talking to John for twenty minutes, the man paid up and drove away in a new Hummer, fully equipped with a rear trailer hitch, a trailer brake controller, a two-and-a-half-ton electric winch, a full rack of fog lights, and a complete stereo sound system.

After less than a year on the job, John was promoted to manager of the used-car sales department. The talk around the shop is that John could sell a refrigerator to an Eskimo. John was indeed a smooth and convincing talker.

John met Rose when she came to the dealership looking to purchase a second car that could handle her wheelchair lift. Although she wanted a small car, John sold her a Chevy Tahoe SUV. John was able to get four of the top mechanics to process the Tahoe. He sold her a 5,000-pound winch, fog lights, a trailer brake controller, a complete stereo system, a DVD movie center, and a fancy GPS.

Rose was so impressed with the way John had handled the sale that she invited him over for dinner. Rose did not cook, but she had a French chef that she had hired away from a restaurant in New Orleans. Rose lived alone in a six-bedroom, five-bathroom mansion, with a three-bedroom, three-bathroom guesthouse on the property, along with a four-bedroom servant's house. All of this rested on a well-kept twenty-five-acre estate.

Rose's family was quite well off. They had the controlling interest in a firm that manufactured chip sets for computers used in system controllers. The firm had the market for these devices all to themselves.

When the economy was strong and the company was doing well, Rose's accountant had estimated her wealth at $4.4 million. In the current weaker economy, her wealth was somewhat less, but she still had plenty. Most of her estate was tied up in company stock, and the value of the stock changed daily.

Although she had a staff of seven employees, Rose was a very lonely person. Rose had a personal aide to take care of her bathing, hairstyling, and general grooming. She had one full-time housekeeper who also did the laundry. Rose's estate also employed a full-time groundskeeper and gardener. An additional part-time gardener rounded out the staff during planting and harvesting times. Rose also liked to grow her own fresh vegetables in her private garden. The chef made meals full time; the chauffeur only worked part time, but he was on call anytime Rose had a need. Rose employed a full-time handyman and maintenance technician as well.

Rose was known to throw some lavish parties just off the rose garden. One day, Rose purchased two nice bathrobes at a fashionable department store. The bathrobes did not have any buttons or zippers, only a cloth belt made from the same material as the robes. When she got home, she threw both belts into the trash can. She invited John over for dinner. After dinner, they played cards until it was quite late. Rose suggested that they both put on the new bathrobes and just rest awhile on her bed.

Rose lay on her back, and of course, her robe came partially open. John's bathrobe still had the price tag attached. John lay on his left side, facing Rose. John's right leg came out of the unfastened robe. He gently lifted his right leg and placed it on top of Rose's bare right leg.

Rose said, "Your leg feels so nice on top of me."

John did not respond to Rose's comment. He did not know what to say, as he had never been this close to four million dollars before. He moved his right hand ever so slowly across her body and placed it on her left thigh. He looked into her eyes, and she just smiled at him. Very slowly, he let his right hand slide up her body until it met her left breast. He gave her breast a gentle squeeze. Again, Rose just gave an approving smile to John. He massaged her nipple with his thumb for two or three strokes, and then, after one more gentle squeeze, they both drifted off to sleep.

About three thirty in the morning, John woke up. He said to Rose, "It's three thirty, and I have to get out of here."

"Not before you have some breakfast," Rose said. She immediately summoned the chef and ordered breakfast for the two of them. The sleepy-eyed chef made a breakfast fit for a king. After breakfast, John got dressed and went on home.

It was not long after this encounter that Rose and John got married.

Rose and John were married under a gazebo on the property. It was a gala event with nearly four hundred guests.

There never was any love in the Cunningham marriage. Rose was very lonely and needed the security of John's presence; John needed Rose as a source of support. Rose never gave any money to John, but she showered him with gifts. John had two motorcycles, a Harley-Davidson Fat Boy and a Honda Gold Wing. He had two cars, a Lamborghini and a red convertible Mustang GT. He also had a cabin cruiser on the lake near the ranch.

Rose did not like the smell of the exhaust from the motorcycles when they started up cold. She said that the smell went all through the house. To solve this problem, she had a two-car detached garage built to house the two motorcycles. The detached garage had a complete overhaul shop for John to play in. When it was time to rebuild his motorcycles, John would bring in a mechanic to do the job right on the premises. If the mechanic needed a tool that John did not have, John just told the mechanic to order it and put it on the bill.

The main house had a four-car garage. Rose has a Toyota minivan with a rear-equipped wheelchair lift. Her Chevy Tahoe had a side-entrance wheelchair lift. Rose's two cars were kept in the main house garage, along with John's Mustang and Lamborghini.

Although there was no love between the two, John would never do anything to upset their weird arrangement.

Rose spent most of her time in the wheelchair. She also had an electric scooter. The wheelchair was much more comfortable than the scooter. She could not maneuver directly from the wheelchair to the scooter or vice versa. What she did was to bring the wheelchair up to her bed. She would then pull herself up by grabbing the bedpost and lying on the bed. She then would roll over to the other side of the bed and slide into the scooter seat by supporting herself with the corner bedpost. It was a lot of work, but she never accepted help for this maneuver. She could do all of this without any outside help. Of course, the reverse process would put her back into the wheel chair.

Rose had contracted polio when she was six years old. It had left her paralyzed from the waist down. She had feelings in her upper legs, but no muscle control whatsoever. Although Rose had servants to help her, she preferred to manage her activities by herself as much as possible.

At that point in the interview, Detective Pulaski said, "Good, all of that is fine ... but tell me, did you push Lisa overboard?"

John said, "Of course not!"

Detective Pulaski said, "Okay. Tell me about your encounter with Lisa after the dance."

"Okay. Lisa was on her way to get a hot chocolate for Phil. We met in the elevator. Another couple rode up in the elevator with us. Lisa and I stopped in the laundry-chute cubbyhole and talked for about forty-five minutes. Then John came and got Lisa, and they went into the twenty-four-hour buffet."

Detective Pulaski said, "And that was the last time you saw Lisa?"

John responded, "Yes, the very last time."

Pulaski queried John further: "Lisa did not come back to your room after she drank her hot chocolate?"

"No, she did not."

"I want to thank you both for your straightforward answers to my questions in this investigation," Detective Pulaski said. "I'll be back later."

Second Cruise, Day 6: Conflicting Information

"Wow! That's some report, Pulaski," was Compton's response. "The boys back at Criminal Records will get a bang out of this one. Good job, Pulaski, good job." Detective Compton paused and then mused, "Looks like we have a little conflict in the testimonies here. According to John, he and Lisa were just talking at the laundry-chute cubbyhole for forty-five minutes. According to Phil, he caught Lisa with her breast exposed and John's head leaning forward, toward Lisa's chest. Better go and get John and bring him up here. Just John—leave Rose there."

John came willingly to the detectives' office. Detective Compton explained the difference in the two testimonies. "You say that you and Lisa were just talking in the laundry-chute cubbyhole, and Phil said he saw Lisa with her breast exposed and your head was bent forward toward Lisa's chest. What say you?"

John replied, "Fellows, I am sorry that I misled you. Rose was in our presence, and I am in enough trouble. If she knew the whole story, it might mean the end of our marriage. What you said about Phil catching us with Lisa's breast exposed is correct. I am sorry for the distortion of the facts."

"Well, that clears that up," Compton said. "Let me ask you, was Phil mad after seeing Lisa standing there with her breast exposed in front of you?"

"I couldn't say. He told Lisa not to come back to their room. Yes, I guess he was mad."

"Phil told Lisa not to go back to their room? Did she go to your room?"

"Lisa has never been to my room," John answered.

"Let me ask you again: did you see Lisa at any time after the laundry-chute cubbyhole encounter?"

"No, I never saw her after she left the cubbyhole."

Compton said, "That will be all. We will call if we need you again."

Compton turned to Pulaski and said, "Let's go and check out some of Phillip Thompson's neighbors."

They first questioned the neighbor next to Phil on the bow side. The man answered the door. Detective Compton introduced himself and Detective Pulaski.

"Are you here to collect money?" the man asked.

Compton replied, "No, we are investigating a homicide case, and we would like to ask you some questions."

The man hollered out, "Dewdrop, there are two guys here to see you."

When the woman began to talk to the detectives, the man went back into the cabin and sat on the couch. Compton asked if they had heard Phil leave his cabin after 10:00 PM.

The man hollered out, "What do they want?"

The lady responded, "Rubin, they want to know if we heard Phil leave his room after 10:00 PM."

Rubin hollered out, "Tell them that we contributed at the church."

"Did you see Lisa leave Phil's room?" Compton asked.

"Dewdrop," Rubin continued, "tell them we don't have any, and not to come back tomorrow." "Rubin, these are detectives investigating a possible murder case."

"Tell them we are innocent," Rubin said.

Dewdrop said, "Rubin, he wants to know if we saw Phil push Lisa overboard."

Rubin said, "We don't push people into the water. We have a .12-gauge shotgun to get rid of bad critters."

Compton and Pulaski thanked both Dewdrop and Rubin for their help in the investigation. Pulaski commented later, "That was a waste of time."

They questioned the passengers next door to Phil on the stern side. The woman said that they had heard everything. Her husband would put his ear against the separating cabin walls, and he could hear everything that was going on in there.

She said, "Phil was a very jealous man. My husband heard him say to Lisa that if she was ever untrue to him, she was to take her little red suitcase and leave. He said this several times. He caught her doing something that she shouldn't, and we think that he pushed her overboard in the middle of the night."

Compton asked, "Are you sure that Phil did not leave the room after 10:05 PM?"

"No," she said.

Her husband agreed, "If Phil left the room, we would have heard it. No, he did not leave." Detectives Compton and Pulaski thanked the neighboring passengers for their help in the investigation.

The neighbors across the passageway confirmed that they thought that Phil was very jealous of Lisa. They also said that Lisa was a very good-looking lady.

Back at the office, Detective Compton said, "Well, partner we have our job cut out for us. Let us lay out what we have. Number one, Phil is a very jealous man. Right?"

"Yes. And John was afraid that Rose would find out about the little goings-on in the laundry-chute cubbyhole."

Compton said, "Looks like we have two suspects with good motives to commit murder. Lisa did not have anyplace to go. She was up the creek, so to speak. She could have been so despondent that she just jumped off the ship."

"Yes," Pulaski said, "but if she jumped, then why did she wave her arm in an effort to be rescued? The little Vietnamese man was quite positive that she wanted to be rescued."

Detective Compton said, "Let's lay out the time frame here. And be sure to get all of this on your recorder, as we will need it for our report back in LA."

"Got it."

Compton continued, "The dance lessons started at 6:30 PM. When the lessons finished at 7:00 PM, the seven-piece band began to play for the main dance. The dance was over at about 9:15 PM. Lisa went with Phil to their room right after the dance. At 9:30 PM, Lisa left Phil's room and went to the buffet for some hot chocolate for the two of them. On her way to the buffet, she met John in the elevator. Lisa and John then went to the laundry-chute cubbyhole, where she exposed her breasts to John, right?"

"That's the way I see it," Pulaski said.

Compton continued, "This happened at about 10:00 PM. John immediately returned to his room and packed Lisa's street clothes into her little red suitcase. This was at about 10:05 PM. At 10:30 PM, the little Vietnamese man spotted Lisa in the water waving her arm for help. Have I got it right so far?"

Pulaski agreed that the story met his understanding of the facts.

Compton said, "Phil testified that he did not leave the room after he returned from the cubbyhole. John testified that he did not leave his room after returning from the cubbyhole. Looks like we have three possibilities here. One: Phil, the jealous lover, pushed Lisa overboard. Two: John, afraid that his affair with Lisa would wreck his marriage, pushed Lisa overboard to keep her quiet. Three: Lisa jumped because there was no other alternative. I simply do not have an opinion. Do you?"

Detective Pulaski responded, "I am afraid not."

Compton's final words were, "This case will probably go down in the journals of unsolved mysteries."

The End

Reader's Survey

The detectives were not able to determine how Lisa got off the ship. If you would like to participate in solving this mystery, please fill out this form, remove it, and send it to the address below. The results of this survey will be published in the back of our new book, *AHRUMPH*.

☐   Lisa was pushed overboard by her jealous lover, Phil.
☐   Lisa was pushed overboard by the married man, John.
☐   Lisa jumped overboard out of sheer desperation.

Duke Tipton
PO Box 473
Sutherlin, Oregon 97479